Found Missing

A Decorah Security Novel

Decorah Security Series, Book #14
A Paranormal Romantic Suspense Novel

By Rebecca York

Ruth Glick writing as Rebecca York

Published by Light Street Press
Copyright © 2016 by Ruth Glick
Cover design by Earthly Charms

This is a work of fiction. Names, characters, places, and
incidents either are the product of the author's imagination
or are used fictitiously, and any resemblance to actual
persons, living or dead, business establishments, events, or
locales is entirely coincidental.

ISBN: 978-1943191031.

PROLOGUE

"Any progress on finding the little bitch?"

The question came from a man with iron-gray hair and a scar that cut across his chin. Leaning back in his comfortable chair, he regarded Carlos Mardano through slitted eyes.

Carlos knew that look. Often it was the prelude to dangerous anger that would flare like boiling lava spewing from a volcano. His boss's dark, hooded eyes were one of the reasons he'd gotten the nickname Rambo. The other was his ruthless pursuit of any goal he set.

Carlos stood a few yards from the man's chair, staring over his shoulder at a weird-looking sketch on the wall. One of the other security guys had told him it was by a big-time artist named Picasso. It was supposed to be an original—and supposed to be expensive, but it looked like someone had taken a face apart and put it back together wrong.

Trying not to think about failure, he pressed his hands to his sides to keep them from trembling. But this whole damn screwup was not his fault. It was a case of shoot the messenger. He'd been off the evening the girl had escaped. He wasn't the one who had been stupid enough to leave car keys lying around. And he sure as hell wasn't the one who had

1

chased her at dangerous speed—then watched her vehicle skid off the road on a sharp turn and plow into a stone wall. Yeah, right. That guy was long dead.

Carlos licked his lips. "We know she was taken to the hospital and admitted as Jane Doe—not Jenny Seaver—because she had no identification. And she was unconscious."

Rambo rocked forward in his chair and let his Gucci loafers slam down on the inlaid parquet floor. "Jesus Christ, you're not telling me anything new. But people don't simply vanish from the hospital."

"Someone checked her out. And whoever let her go tampered with the paperwork. There's no record of her having even been there."

"Yeah, well, something weird is going on. I want to know who took her away, what they did with her, and why."

Despite the air conditioning in the room, Carlos felt sweat collect at the back of his neck and trickle down the inside of his shirt. "I did some snooping around the administrative offices. I think the hospital was glad to get rid of her because she had no insurance, as far as they knew. So who was going to pay the bills of some no-name chick in a coma?"

Rambo pushed himself up straighter. "Probably somebody was paid to take her off their hands. I want you to find out who it was—and I want them brought here for interrogation."

The younger man shuddered, thinking about the holding cells in the basement below the high-class rooms on the house's main floor. People went down the steps to the lower level and never came out again—at least under their own power.

He wanted to ask, "What if she's dead?" But he kept the question locked behind his lips. If she was dead, that might be the same as failing to find her.

"Go on. Get busy."

Thankful to escape, Carlos turned on his heel. As he exited the wood-paneled office, he heard the boss muttering, "If that bitch has fucked up my plans, I'll kill her."

Carlos hurried down the corridor and into the sunshine, where he stood on the back patio taking gulps of air. He didn't much like the position he was in now. But at least he wasn't Jenny Seaver. He remembered the girl as a complete wimp. Who would believe she had the balls to escape?

And now she was missing, probably badly injured. It still amazed him that she'd managed to run away, but her unlikely escape only spoke of her desperation.

Where the hell was she? And how long did he have to find her before the boss went batshit and struck out at the wrong target?

CHAPTER ONE

She'd had the foresight to call herself Jenny Seville, not Jenny Seaver when she'd first arrived here. The assumed name had helped her feel less conspicuous. Now she was a lot more at ease in this place. Dressed in comfortable stretch jeans and a sunny yellow tee shirt, she walked across the grounds of the Mirador Hotel, smiling as she took in the lush greenery, the tropical flowers, and the high wall that marked the edge of the property.

Above her the sky was a brilliant blue, set off by a few fluffy clouds drifting lazily in a light breeze. Not thunderheads, because it only rained here at two o'clock in the morning on Tuesdays.

The complex practically defined lavish excess. The public areas were filled with priceless art from around India. Each luxury room overflowed with comfortable furniture and fine antiques. The dining room had anything you might want to eat. The exercise facilities were top of the line. And there were even features installed especially to accommodate requests she'd made.

She stopped for a moment beside the Olympic-sized pool bounded by a wide deck of concrete and Moorish ceramic tiles, then continued on to a new building that was quite different from the rest of the venue.

Pulling open a heavy door, she stepped inside a room that was about thirty feet long and about twenty feet wide. At the far end was a floor-to-ceiling projection screen so that the wall could be transformed into any scene stored in the computer.

Familiar with the setup, Jenny picked up one of the specially modified Sig Sauer automatic pistols lying on a table near the door and checked to make sure it was ready for action. When she saw that it had a full charge, she brushed her chestnut hair back from her face and pressed the activation switch on the simulator unit. Immediately she was facing a scene that she had never seen before. The screen at the far end of the room showed a parking lot, but it was so real she might actually have been there. From where she stood, she saw a man approaching his car about fifteen yards away. Just as he reached it, another guy sprinted over, a gun in his hand.

At first glance, it looked like a clear case of one man getting ready to rob the other, but she'd seen a lot of these scenarios, and she knew they weren't always what you thought.

As she watched, the first guy whirled, gun in hand, and pumped several shots into the dude who had been coming after him. As the wounded man fell to the ground, the one still standing pivoted toward her, his malevolent gaze like a silent curse. Instinctively she fired, but not before she felt a hot jolt of pain in her left shoulder. Despite the simulated hit, she kept pulling the trigger. The guy went down, and she was left standing in the parking lot with two crumpled bodies. Her arm throbbed for a few more seconds before the injury miraculously evaporated as though nothing had happened.

She looked at the scene of carnage, analyzing what had just gone down. Apparently the first guy had been the robber and the second one had been rushing after him to get his property back. She had been assigned the part of an undercover cop.

Although she hadn't been fast enough to avoid getting shot, she had felled the bad guy.

Turning to the console, she pressed the button to wipe away the scene and cue up another scenario. This time she was driving a car in a line of vehicles on a crowded road. Directly in front of her she could see a cute young woman in a late model sedan. In front of her car was a police van. The woman looked perfectly innocent, only it turned out that she was there to spring the prisoner in the back of the police transport. In the shoot-out that ensued, Jenny ended up with a bullet in the chest, thankful that the effects lasted only a few seconds.

She did better in the next confrontation when she walked in on a man stealing drugs from a hospital pharmacy.

The training was intense as always, with scenarios where you had to decide in seconds whether you were facing a criminal or an innocent bystander. After forty-five minutes of life or death decision- making, she turned off the equipment and put the gun back where she'd found it.

In the session, she'd gained some good insights into criminal behavior and into her own ability to react in an emergency. In this shooting gallery, she hadn't hesitated to kill. But could she shoot someone in the real world? She couldn't help thinking that she would get the chance to find out. And one thing she knew for sure—she had a lot more confidence in her ability to defend herself than when she'd first come to the Mirador.

Leaving the indoor training area, she walked to a secluded part of the hotel lawn where Art Landon, the guy who ran this place, had constructed an obstacle course for her. She worked her way around the setups, climbing a rope, jumping into a sandpit, scaling a wall, then wiggling through a series of body-sized rubber pipes that made her feel claustrophobic.

Finally as a reward for all the hard work, she stopped by the pottery studio that Art had also provided for her. She had many artistic talents, but she'd chosen to focus on her ceramic skills while she was at the Mirador. Yesterday she'd glazed and fired some decorative pots, and now she took them out of the kiln, critically inspecting her craftsmanship before setting them on shelves at the side of the studio. Working with clay was a skill she'd acquired before coming to the Mirador, but she was definitely improving her technique. Too bad she couldn't take any of these pieces with her when she left.

Pushing that thought out of her mind, she headed for the pool where she'd left her suit in one of the private cabanas. After putting it on, she turned to the small computer unit where she brought up a list of music selections and chose a medley of operatic arias that she particularly liked. As Kathleen Battle began to sing a lament from *Don Giovanni*, Jenny walked to the deep end of the pool where she executed a perfect dive into the warm water. It felt good, but should it be a couple of degrees cooler? Perhaps she should speak to Landon about that. In her mind, she thought of him as the maintenance man. But he was so much more—the skilled computer operator who kept this place running, which was a lot more work than keeping the bushes trimmed and the walks swept.

When she surfaced, she began to swim back toward the cabanas, cutting through the water with long, graceful strokes. At the far end, she turned and started back the way she'd come, keeping a steady pace.

For a few minutes, she let the water and the physical activity soothe her, but when Sarah Brightman started to sing "Time to Say Goodbye," she faltered in the water. It was one of her favorite concert arias, but it reminded her again that she couldn't stay here forever. She could keep training and building up her defensive skills, but for how long? Surely she was putting all the other residents here in danger—if the wrong people came looking for her. My God, what if something happened to sweet little Shelly—the only child in residence at the hotel? And what about Grant Bradley?

Grant didn't live here, but he came to the Mirador often. He'd showed her how to operate the shooting scenarios and given her pointers on how to use them. He'd worked with Landon to design the obstacle course for her. And he'd taken her to the outdoor firing range for target practice, using not only handguns but assault rifles. He had recognized her initial lack of self-confidence and done everything he could to build up her defensive skills.

But she knew the time he spent with her wasn't just about a training program. Grant was attracted to her. And she was to him. That didn't mean it was easy to deal with their relationship. She'd vowed to maintain the barrier she'd put up between them, because no matter how much she wanted to trust him, she couldn't entirely let down her guard. Not after what had happened the last time she'd allowed herself to be vulnerable to a man.

In the water she balled her hands into fists. Sooner than later she would have to face—and say good-bye. To the Mirador Hotel—and to Grant.

When Grant Bradley stepped into the advanced medical center being maintained under the auspices of Decorah Security, his brother, Mack, was sitting at the front desk watching computer screens that gave him multiple views of the facility.

His twin gave him a questioning look. "You aren't on duty now."

"No, I'm just stopping by."

When Mack gave him a knowing look, Grant kept his gaze steady. His brother didn't have to read his mind to know why he was here.

Raised in rural Western Maryland the brothers were near identical twins. Both were tall and dark haired with the lean builds of men who had always enjoyed outdoor pursuits and athletics. The clue to telling them apart was that Mack kept his hair military short and Grant had a slightly longer cut. Mack had attended the Naval Academy and become a pilot.

After college, Grant had joined the CIA, gotten disillusioned with The Agency, and gone back to running their dad's outfitter business.

Both of them were now with Decorah Security. Mack was currently assigned full-time to the specialized medical unit. Grant was on a rotating staff of agents who pulled part-time duty there.

"You're going to take another crack at getting Jenny Seville to talk?"

"Yeah."

His brother looked sympathetic. "Good luck with that. Haven't you been trying for months?"

"I've been making sure she feels like she can take care of herself. She was glad to focus on defense training, but she's been avoiding talking about her problem."

"She still doesn't trust you?" Mack asked.

"Only so far. Not enough to tell me how she ended up at the Mirador."

"You can't force information out of her," Mack said.

"Yeah, and if I push her—I could drive her farther away."

Leaving his brother, Grant walked down the hall to the main patient area, where Lily Wardman looked up from her computer station. She was his brother's wife and also the doctor in charge.

Behind her were twelve specially designed beds, most occupied by patients who had been unconscious since before they'd arrived here.

As always Grant felt his chest tighten when he looked toward the bed where Jenny Seville was lying. Like all the patients here, she had been part of a medical experiment formerly operated by Dr. Philip Hamilton. Hamilton had hooked her and the others up to a computer feed that immersed them in a virtual reality. Instead of simply lying unconscious in specially designed hospital beds, they were experiencing a full and very active life in a five-star hotel in India.

Hamilton had been so eager to try out his theories with comatose patients that he'd obtained many of them by questionable means. Lily Wardman had originally worked for Hamilton, not knowing he was bending medical ethics and the law to populate his experiment with warm bodies.

After Hamilton had been arrested, Lily had taken over the operation under the auspices of Decorah Security, which now ran the medical center for the benefit of the patients.

Before Grant could stop himself, he blurted the question that was always on his mind, "Any change in Jenny's status?"

"As a matter of fact, I have observed something new."

His whole body tensed. "Is she worse? And you haven't wanted to tell me?"

"No. Actually, she's very close to full consciousness. There have been signs for the past couple of weeks. She's opened her eyes and looked at me. And I'm pretty sure she's heard me talking to her."

"Like Mack," he said. His brother, who had been cleared for duty at the security desk, had been one of the patients illegally obtained for Dr. Hamilton's lab. And when the facility had been under attack, he'd been able to wake himself up and help with the defense. Knowing that his brother had made a full recovery gave Grant hope that Jenny could do the same.

"Then why isn't she conscious?" he asked now.

Before Lily could answer, he hurried to Jenny, where she lay in the special bed that kept her muscles toned and her skin healthy. Her eyes were closed, her arms at her sides, a blank expression on her delicate features. When he was with her in the VR, she was totally different—alive and well and full of vitality. Here, she was a shadow of what she could be.

"Jenny?"

She didn't respond.

Lily had come up beside him. "I think she's resisting rejoining the real world."

"Can't you—give her something?"

"I could, but I think it's better if we don't interfere with the natural process. Mack is lucky that he made the transition without any serious problems."

Grant clamped his teeth together, then made an effort to relax his jaw.

"I'm going in there to talk to her."

"It's not that good for you to keep putting yourself under."

He swiveled his head toward her. "You go in to see your sister, Shelly." The girl had been in a coma since a long-ago car accident. In the VR she looked like a six-year-old child—which was her mental age. But in reality her body was that of a woman in her twenties.

He waited for Lily to say, "That's different."

Instead, she closed her eyes for a moment before giving him a sympathetic look. "Okay."

"Thank you. Where is she?"

"She used the shooting scenario simulation, ran the obstacle course, and got in some practice at the firing range, then went to her pottery studio."

"That's good. She's keeping busy."

"Now she's in the pool."

"Okay, thanks." He went into the dressing room, took off his clothes, and put on one of the patient gowns. When he returned, Lily directed him to one of the empty beds that they used for visitors to the VR. Once he had lain down, she expertly attached an IV line to his arm and started the drip. Moments later, he was in a room off the lobby of the Mirador Hotel.

He lay for a moment on the couch in the windowless lounge area, orienting himself. Then he swung his legs to the floor and looked around. The transition was familiar, yet it was always amazing to him that he could flit from the real world to this perfectly designed artificial one so easily—and come back when he wanted to.

As always when he arrived, he was wearing the standard running suit patients were issued until they changed into something they liked better.

When he stepped out the door, he was struck again by the cunning reality of the place.

In effect, it was like leaping into a beautiful alternate reality. Or maybe like traveling to the other side of the globe without having to take a plane. Every detail of this hotel in Agra, India, was accurate, down to the veins in the marble floor and the vase of red roses on the check-in desk.

The first few times he'd come to the hotel, there had been no one manning the desk. In fact, except for the guests, the place had looked like a ghost hotel. Now an attractive dark-haired woman dressed in an expensive-looking silk sari stood behind the counter. He knew that instead of being "real," she was part of the setting—programmed into the computer that ran the virtual reality.

"Can I help you?" she asked in a lilting Indian accent.

"I'm here to see Jenny Seville."

"I'll just check to make sure your entry is authorized," she said, bending to a computer screen.

"Fine." He waited impatiently while she verified his access.

"Have a nice day."

"I hope so. Is Jenny still at the pool?"

The woman consulted her computer again. "I believe so."

"Thanks," he said, thinking it was odd to be having such a normal-sounding exchange with a woman who could be erased from existence by a few keystrokes.

He walked to the lobby shop—another feature that had been added to the original program. Inside he found the men's wear section, selected a pair of bathing trunks, and brought them with him as he exited onto one of the airy colonnades that led to various outdoor venues around the hotel. He could see Jenny's shooting gallery in the distance and another building that functioned as a winter resort, using similar technology. It had been provided for Chris Morgan, a ski instructor who was one of the residents.

As Grant hurried toward the pool, his pulse began to pound in his ears, almost blotting out the opera music drifting toward him. And his heart skipped a beat when he saw Jenny, cutting expertly through the water. She looked strong and lithe.

He stepped into one of the cabanas, took off his running suit, and pulled on the trunks. Then he strode to the shallow end of the pool, slipping in quietly and moving to the center so that Jenny almost collided with him as she reached the side.

She blinked when she realized who had interrupted her solitary swim, then stood. A welcoming smile flickered on her lips before she brought her features to neutral and backed a few feet away.

"Hi," he said, meaning to sound casual, but he heard the thickness of his voice.

"Hi," she answered, looking like she wished he hadn't shown up. "What are you doing here?"

"You don't sound glad to see me."

"That's not true," she contradicted.

"Good. I thought we could talk."

"About what?" she asked cautiously.

"I want you to let me help you."

"You have. All the training I've been doing has made me feel ... a lot more confident."

After delivering the assurance, she looked down at the water, and he could see her withdrawing into a private space where he couldn't reach her.

"Jenny?"

Jenny raised her head, her gaze not quite steady. She and Grant had first met when the VR was under attack by an unknown force, and she'd been afraid to trust him or anyone else. The facility was safe now, and she was no longer the same scared woman who had thought the Mirador Hotel was the perfect bolt-hole.

But even as Grant had helped her boost her self-confidence, she'd kept a barrier between them. It was partly because she didn't want him to get hurt. And partly because she simply couldn't let down her guard. But as he stood facing her today in the pool, she knew something had changed between them. Or more accurately she had changed, and she was going to reach for what she had wanted for too long.

She took a step closer, seeing the surprise in his eyes. He said her name again, as she reached for him. When his arms came up to fold her into his embrace, she sighed and closed her eyes, blocking out everything except the man who held her water-slick body against his. When he gathered her closer, she leaned into him, no longer able to deny the needs and emotions that had been building within her.

"Thank God," he growled, the words barely above a whisper before his lips came down on hers, his large hands stroking up and down her back. When he cupped her bottom she felt herself pulled against the rigid flesh straining at the front of his bathing trunks.

She had lived like a nun the whole time she had been at the Mirador Hotel. No more. And she knew he was tuned to the responses she had struggled to hold in check.

He made a low sound deep in his chest as he played with the straps of her bathing suit, slipping his hands underneath to caress the skin of her shoulders and then the tops of her breasts.

Had she ever felt anything as exquisite as the stroking of his fingers against her wet skin?

The touch was light, but it set her body on fire. She forgot her own warning, forgot everything but his taste—his touch. And her own swelling response.

Her breasts ached. The nipples especially. They had contracted painfully, and the only way she could ease the tight sensation was to press them against his chest.

That was no help. It only made her crave more. And then more.

She felt desperation rising inside her. Not the desperation to escape that had sent her hurtling from the people who were holding her captive back in her old life.

This was a desperation to finally get as close as she could to Grant Bradley.

When the kiss broke, she raised her head, looking around in a daze.

"We're out in the open," she managed to say.

"Yeah."

Under the water, he knitted his fingers with hers, leading her to the wide steps he'd come down. He guided her up to the pool deck, then to one of the cabanas. Glad to let him take the lead, she followed him beyond the curtains to the semidarkness of the interior. There was a chaise inside, this one double width, with the back folded down to make a bed, as though someone had known she and Grant would be coming here.

He turned to her, murmuring her name against her mouth, nibbling with his lips and then his teeth. Her whole body throbbed to the contact. Still, part of her was standing back, watching the two of them together, unable to quite believe that this was really happening.

"I've wanted you for so long. I thought you didn't want me," he murmured as he aroused her.

"You were wrong," she answered, amazed that she could say the words out loud.

"Then why did you keep me at arm's length?"

"I was trying to keep you safe." And *myself*, she silently added.

"From what?"

"My ghosts," she managed to answer.

To stop the conversation going any farther, she brought her mouth back to his for a heated kiss. To her relief he didn't try to get more information out of her, probably because he was as overwhelmed as she by this physical contact. She was the one who had reached for him in the pool, but now he was sweeping her along with him to some dark, dangerous place that she hardly recognized. A place where she felt out of control. And reckless. And on the verge of pleasure only he could give her.

CHAPTER TWO

She would not be denied this moment, Jenny told herself. No, she wouldn't deny it to either one of them.

As she clung to Grant, she could feel his erection through the thin fabric of her bathing suit and his trunks. She wanted to move against it, and when she did, he made sounds of approval.

She was wearing a modest two-piece suit. He reached for the lower edge of the top, slipped his hands inside and pulled it up and over her head so that they were suddenly both naked to the waist. Her nipples tightened as his hot gaze traveled over her breasts.

"Lord, you're gorgeous," he said, his voice not quite steady as he pulled her close enough to slide her upper body against his, the exquisite sensations making it difficult to breathe.

When he went still, her eyes blinked open, and she caught the intensity of his gaze.

"You're sure about this?"

"Can't you tell?"

"I want to hear you say it."

No more hiding, she told herself as she raised her gaze to his. "I want you—now."

He clasped more tightly, and they rocked together, hands stroking wet flesh as they exchanged open-mouth kisses.

He slipped his hands inside the top of her shorts, dragging them over her hips and down her legs.

She kicked them away, moving closer as she reached into the sides of his bathing trunks, caressing his hips and his butt, hearing his indrawn breath as she stroked him. She had been raised to be careful about her associations and her behavior. She hadn't even been allowed to date until late in her teens, and she was very conscious that she was stepping over a line by going this far with a man who hadn't been vetted by her father.

Yet none of the old rules applied. Her family had let her down in a way that she was still trying to comprehend.

To hell with them. And what was wrong with what she was doing, anyway? This wasn't even the real world. She was just grateful that she was here—in this place—with Grant Bradley.

Determined to show herself—and him—that there was no going back, she dragged his trunks over his hips, so that he was suddenly as naked as she.

With her head resting on his shoulder, she stroked her hands over his hips and butt again, glorying in the feel of his water-slick skin.

His erection pressed against her stomach. But that wasn't where she needed to feel him.

He knew it too, because he moved back against the wall of the cabana, splaying his legs to equalize their height and cupping her bottom to bring her hot, swollen sex against his penis. His other hand moved to her breast, tugging and squeezing one nipple, the sensations reinforcing and magnifying each other.

"Oh, God," she gasped, unable to stop herself from moving against him, faster and faster until a small explosion shuddered through her.

When it subsided, her eyes blinked open, and she found him watching her.

Now her face was flaming. "I'm sorry."

"About what?"

"About coming undone like that," she managed to whisper.

"I liked watching you," he answered. "I liked making you so hot that you went up in flames."

"But you ..."

"I think we can take care of me," he answered. "As soon as you're ready to come again."

The frank way he said it made her face heat a few degrees more, even when she told herself there was nothing wrong with the two of them being honest with each other—at least as honest as she could be.

He scooped her up in his arms and laid her on the chaise, then came down beside her, gathering her close as he began to explore her body more intimately. He kissed her mouth, then trailed his lips down to the collarbone, tasting her there before moving down to her breast, circling her nipple with his tongue, then sucking it into his mouth.

She gasped with pleasure, then gasped again as his hand slid downward into the slick folds of her sex, dipping into her vagina, circling inside her before sliding up to her clit to circle her again.

And all the time he was watching her, watching her face. She let go of long-ingrained inhibitions as she began to move her hips, increasing the friction of his hand while he stroked her most intimate flesh.

Her breath came in quick gasps, and she knew she was building to another shuddering climax. And he knew it too.

"Open your legs."

She did as he asked, feeling his body covering hers and his penis pressing against her opening, then pushing into her. Clasping his shoulders, she held on to him.

She was prepared for him to grab his own pleasure now—leaving her wanting. Instead, he moved slowly, centered on her reactions, moving in and out of her in long, slow strokes until the building sensations became her focus.

His care with her was glorious. He shifted their bodies to the side so that he could caress her breasts while he built her arousal. It wasn't until she felt the first tremors of climax that he quickened his pace, pushing for his own satisfaction as he drove her over the edge, into a world that was all blinding white sensation.

She felt his hot seed spurt into her, heard his shout of completion as he anchored her in his arms, and she dug her fingers into his back, holding him to her, glorying in the wonder of the moment.

The pinnacle of her satisfaction had been astonishing. And afterwards was almost as good. Grant kept her in his arms, and she snuggled against him.

She had wanted to be with him like this forever—since she'd realized he wasn't being nice to her because he felt obligated.

"If I'd known it was going to be that good, maybe I wouldn't have resisted for so long," she whispered.

"Uh huh."

"Did I say that out loud?"

"Yeah."

He kept her with him, cradling her naked body against his side, his lips nibbling her cheek, his hands stroking over her heated skin, and she would have been content to stay there forever.

"Thank you," she murmured. Then a thought occurred to her, and she felt a little shudder go through her.

Grant felt it, too. "What's wrong?"

"I'm thinking about Lily back in the lab."

"What about her?"

"She must have seen my ... I don't know. Heart rate and breathing spike."

"Mine too. I guess she knows that whatever we were doing—we were doing it together."

"Yes."

"Do you care?"

"I should."

"Why?"

She heard herself say, "Because I was raised in a very strict environment—where I was expected to maintain high standards of behavior."

"And your background has something to do with why you're in trouble?"

"Yes," she answered again, wishing she hadn't gotten trapped in this conversation.

She moved out of his arms, immediately missing the contact and also feeling very naked. Looking around for something to wear, she spotted her wet bathing suit lying on the tile floor.

He saw at once that she was uncomfortable.

"Back in a flash."

He got up, apparently unconcerned with his nudity and moved to a hanging rack at the side of the cabana where he took down two terry robes. She pulled one on, and he donned the other before lying beside her on the chaise again.

"Better than that wet suit."

She nodded, but nudity wasn't the worst of her problems. Struggling for honesty, she said, "I feel like you've tricked me into talking about myself."

She knew the remark had gotten to him by the way hurt flashed across his features. "You think I made love with you to get you to talk?"

"No. I think that making love was something we both wanted for a long time."

"I did. But I didn't want to push you. And then in the pool, you reached for me."

She dragged in a breath and let it out. "But even when we've just been intimate, you can't stop being an investigator."

He laughed, then sobered again. "I guess that's right. But even now, you can't stop yourself from keeping secrets from me. Don't you trust me?"

21

"I wouldn't have gone to bed with you if I didn't trust you."

"But only so far."

His perception was like a quick stab wound.

When he saw the pain on her face, he reached for her and pulled her close again. With a sigh, she settled down beside him, wishing everything were simple. A long time ago, her life had seemed uncomplicated. Too bad that nothing in her recent experience was easy.

And too bad he wasn't going to stop probing. "You grew up on a big estate, didn't you?" he asked suddenly.

"How did you know?" she managed to ask.

"I didn't. Not for sure. But I saw the way you took this luxurious hotel in stride. Not like some of the other residents who were wide-eyed at the opulence."

"Am I that transparent?"

"No. Like you said, I'm a good ... observer. But I'm on your side. I'm hoping you can trust me with the secrets you've been hiding since you got here," he pressed.

"I want to," she answered.

"Then open up with me."

Not now. Don't push me now. Those words churned in her mind. What she said was, "Give me a little time." As she made the plea, she held her breath, hoping that the answer would satisfy him.

"Okay."

She had just allowed herself to relax in his arms again when he said, "I talked to Lily about you before I came in."

On guard again, she asked, "About what?"

"She says that you're close to waking up. But she thinks you're keeping yourself from doing it."

It wasn't exactly true. She knew she was close to waking up, and she was hoping to choose the time when she climbed out of the special bed she'd been occupying for the past few months. But she wasn't going to explain that to Grant or admit her motives.

"I'll be there when you wake up," he said.

"I know," she answered, hoping she sounded like she wanted that to be true. Changing the subject completely, she asked, "Do you think that in here we can make love as much as we want? I mean more than people can in ... reality."

"Maybe we should find out," he answered, slipping his hand inside her robe, caressing her breasts.

She knew he wasn't going to keep questioning her now, and she welcomed her response to him again, silently thanking him for the chance to spend a little more quality time together.

CHAPTER THREE

More than once, Carlos Mardano had thought about leaving Rambo's employment—not with a formal two weeks' notice but by sneaking away late some evening. He could pretend he was going out to get a pack of cigarettes, leave all his clothes and possessions here, and just keep driving. But he knew it was a mistake to simply walk out on a man like his boss. The man was a hard case. And he held grudges. He'd kept searching for guys who had dissed him years ago—and made them pay for the insult. That knowledge had kept Carlos digging for information about Jenny Seaver long after he would have given up.

Now he stood in front of Rambo's desk, trying not to shift his weight from foot to foot or slide his damp palms along his hips. He'd been hired as a muscle man, for shit's sake, not a researcher. Yet he'd been beating the bushes for any news of the girl. And maybe finally he'd found an opening they could use.

"I think I have something for you," he said.

He watched his boss lean forward expectantly, watched his hooded eyes narrow.

Carlos cleared his throat. "Jenny Seaver was admitted to St. Luke's hospital in a coma. It was going to be expensive to take care of her. Plus they were doubtful about her chances of waking up. So they were thinking about pulling the plug."

Anger flashed in Rambo's eyes. "You're not telling me she's dead?"

"No." Carlos was quick to correct that impression. "After she'd been there a couple of days, a guy named Dr. Philip Hamilton showed up and said he could take her off their hands."

"For what reason?"

"He said he had a research project aimed at improving the lives of comatose patients."

"How do you do that?"

"I didn't get any details. Apparently the Hamilton guy was desperate for subjects to use in his project. He came back in a fancy-ass ambulance and took her away."

"To another hospital?"

"No. A lab—the Hamilton Lab."

"Where?"

"In Bethesda, Maryland."

Rambo kept his laser gaze on Carlos. "And you know all this how?"

"I got it from one of the orderlies working in the unit. He heard the conversation."

"He's reliable?"

"He didn't have any reason to lie. And I paid him for the information."

"Okay. Then we know where the little bitch is."

Carlos cleared his throat, bracing for his boss's displeasure. "Not exactly."

A dangerous anger flashed in Rambo's eyes. "What the hell does that mean—exactly?"

"Apparently, it wasn't a strictly legit operation. Or at least, the doctor was getting patients—like Jenny—illegally. There was some kind of dustup, and the FBI put the lab out of business."

"You're saying there were other patients involved besides Jenny?"

"Yes."

"You can't hide a bunch of people whose brains are whacked up. Find out what the hell happened to them—to her."

"You want me to go down to DC and poke around?"

"Of course. What do you think, you idiot?"

Carlos left, thanking his luck that he'd escaped Rambo's wrath once more. Too bad the lab had been illegal. Too bad it had been closed—with no official forwarding address. But how could they have shut it down when there were a bunch of zombies involved?

Well, he knew the previous location. That was a start. And maybe the patients were still in the local area. Were they still all together? Or had they been scattered around like furniture from an apartment where the tenant had been evicted?

He guessed the first place to start was with the staff. Hamilton couldn't have been running an operation like that on his own. He needed orderlies, nurses, maybe even another doctor. Were they still in the Bethesda area? Had they moved away, and were they working at the new lab?

He clenched his fists, hating this whole situation.

Rambo had called Jenny Seaver a little bitch. Carlos wished the crash had killed her. Then he'd be off the hook. Like the old lady who used to lurk around the place. She was Rambo's sister, and she'd loved lording it over the staff. But she'd vanished around the same time Jenny had escaped. Or that was the official story.

Maybe it hadn't been as smooth a departure as Rambo had intimated.

Carlos shuddered, thinking that you couldn't take anything for granted around this place.

CHAPTER FOUR

Because Jenny felt weird about the other residents of the VR knowing she might have been intimate with Grant, she asked him to return to the hotel ahead of her. She hadn't wanted to send him away, but she had things to do. And one good point about living in this place was that you could really operate twenty-hour hours a day, if you wanted.

After finding her clothing in the next cabana, she showered, dressed and blew her hair dry, thinking how strange it was that she could do everything here that she could in the real world.

When she came back up the path, Paula Rendell, who had been a travel agent before ending up in the VR, was outside sitting in front of an easel and painting the bougainvillea on the wall. Jenny waited for her to make a comment about Grant, but if she'd noticed him returning from the pool, she kept the observation to herself.

Jenny felt a pang as she stopped to admire the woman's work. Paula was one of the residents who was never getting out of the VR because her brain injury was too serious. But here she could have a reasonable life. Since both of them were artists, they'd talked about their work. Paula had come to Jenny's pottery studio, and Jenny went out of her way to comment on Paula's work.

"You're getting really good," she said as she studied the lifelike rendering of the vivid magenta flowers. Jenny had also done a lot of painting herself before focusing on pottery. But that was in another life—like all of the other activities she'd thrown herself into.

"Thanks."

Jenny couldn't stop from asking, "Do you wish that other people could see your paintings? I mean have a gallery show or something."

Paula laughed. "I'm not that good."

"I think you will be," Jenny answered. In her previous life, she'd been exposed to lots of good art, and she was confident of her judgment.

"Thanks so much. But I'm just grateful to be able to do it at all."

Jenny nodded, glad she had more options than Paula but at the same time worried about her choices. If she made the wrong one, it wouldn't only affect her.

"The scenery's limited, though," Jenny said.

Paula nodded. "But Art is willing to expand the environment. I asked him to set up some views for me. I mean, like he did with your shooting scenario room and Chris's ski slopes. I'm starting with a villa I visited in Tuscany. I can click a button and have a virtual tour."

"Clever idea."

"I got it from you."

Jenny grinned. "Glad I could help."

Paula gave her a considering look. "You've changed since you've been here. I remember when you didn't even want to tell us your name—or where you came from."

Jenny swallowed. Really, it was still true. But apparently she'd talked enough about herself to fit in to this little makeshift community.

After a few more minutes, Jenny headed for the hotel again. When she stepped into the lobby, she glanced at the clock over the front desk. It said, 5:00 PM, which meant very little here. But most of the residents did note the hours, to maintain a normal tenor to their days.

The sari-clad woman at the desk looked up. "Did you have a nice workout?"

Jenny flushed. She'd had a very nice workout, but she wasn't going to talk about it. Of course, the woman wasn't real. She was just part of the computer program, and Jenny told herself it was silly to be embarrassed by a question asked by a simulacrum.

"Um hum," she answered, then headed for one of the offices off the lobby. Inside was a desk with a communications terminal that had several purposes. Hotel residents could use the Web, send and receive e-mail, contact the outside staff, or just look in on the patient area—which is what Jenny chose to do now.

Most of the patients at the hotel, like Paula, seemed content to live here without worrying about the environment. That made sense because most of them had injuries that would keep them from functioning in the real world. Their best option was to relax and enjoy the Mirador.

But Jenny was different. After Lily had taken over running the lab, she'd spoken to each of the residents about their prognosis. She'd told Jenny she had a good chance of waking up, and Jenny had been preparing herself for that eventuality ever since.

Because of that, she'd been keeping track of the VR project. Now as she switched to a view of the lab, she saw Lily talking to one of the Bradley brothers. To most people, they were hard to tell apart. But she knew it was Grant.

There were subtle differences between the two of them. Like the way their hair was cut. Grant's was a little longer than Mack's. And she knew that Grant, who'd taken over their dad's outfitter business, was more likely to be wearing blue jeans than his brother who still had a more military style of dress, even though he was now out of the Navy. She couldn't suppress a little laugh. Out of the Navy because he was officially dead.

There were several settings for the monitor. At the moment, the sound was off, and her end of the connection was blank. She kept herself from being seen as she turned up the sound so she could hear what was going on.

Since she'd arrived in the middle of a conversation, it took a moment to orient herself.

"When is he coming?" Grant asked.

"Tomorrow. And I want you on hand to help out."

Mack stepped into the picture. "What's the problem?"

"I don't think there's necessarily going to be one, but I want to take precautions when we introduce a new patient to the VR," Lily answered.

"Agreed," both men said.

"Who is he?" Mack asked.

"A guy named Jonas Corker. He was injured in a warehouse accident."

"And why are you taking him on?"

Lily turned to her husband, her facial expression controlled. But Jenny knew she was good at hiding her real emotions. She'd been in the VR, pretending to be a patient when everyone had awakened here for the first time. Back then, Dr. Hamilton had wanted to see how they'd react to waking up in a strange environment, which had led to a lot of speculation and stress in the group. Jenny was pretty sure Lily wasn't going to hide the purpose of the VR from someone new coming in. But that didn't mean that introducing him was necessarily going to go smoothly.

"We're a Decorah Security operation now, and my mandate from Frank Decorah is to admit new patients who would significantly improve the quality of their lives by having access to the VR."

"How do you know he'll fit in?" Mack pressed.

30

"I can't know for sure, but I've studied his medical records and his background. From what I can gather, he was a normal, stable guy before he had some bad luck at work."

"Okay."

"You're worried about letting him in?" Lily asked her husband.

"I'm remembering that Jay Douglas attacked you when he first woke up in there. He would have hurt you if I hadn't shown up. He was unstable. Hamilton never should have acquired him for the program,"

Lily winced at the word acquired.

"In fact, Hamilton wasn't doing much vetting of anybody, as I remember," Mack continued. "He stole me and tried to pretend I was dead."

Lily sighed. "I'm trying to be a lot more ethical—and a lot more cautious, but I can't guarantee a hundred percent that there won't be problems. Which is why I want one of you to be present when I tell him what's going on."

It looked like Mack wanted to say something, but Lily held up her hand and plowed ahead. "Plus, I've taken an additional precaution. For the safety of the patient population already living in the hotel, I've set up a safe room—one of the offices off the lobby, only I've had Art arrange it like a small living room. Jonas will wake up on the sofa. You'll be on another sofa when I wake him up."

"Okay," Mack said, but Jenny could tell that he still wasn't entirely happy with the arrangement.

"And I'll be monitoring the situation out here," Grant said.

"Along with Art," Lily added. "I can stay in constant communication with him, and if we need to, Art can bring Jonas back to his bed in the lab."

The conversation about the new patient went on for several more minutes, with each of the twins making additional suggestions. But finally the matter was settled. After the men had left, Jenny continued to view the scene, this time focusing on the layout of the lab.

She could see her own bed, the other patients, the exit—
and the desk that Lily used plus the door to the dressing
room where they changed clothes when they were going into
the VR. It was like watching a security camera with a
continuous feed.

As Jenny clicked off, she was thinking that she was never
going to have a better chance to get away from this
environment without Dr. Wardman's knowing about it for
several hours.

One thing Lily had told her was that there was a
correlation between the physical training Jenny was doing in
the VR and her physical condition in the real world. The
special bed she was lying in was toning her body. But her
own efforts to up her fitness level were adding to the effect.

Even with all the effort Jenny was putting in, Lily had
cautioned her that she wasn't going to be back to her old self
until she'd done a lot of physical therapy. But she knew that
Mack had made himself function quickly when he'd had to do
it. And she wasn't going to let any man show her up.

She smiled to herself. If she could think something like
that, she had come a long way from the passive woman who
had fled unexpected captivity. Then she'd felt like she had no
choice. Now she was about to take a step that scared her.
But not in the old, helpless way. She might be scared, but
she wasn't going to let that stop her.

She opened the door to the computer room and looked
out. The lobby was empty except for the woman attendant,
and Jenny was glad not to see Tom Wright. A used car
salesman with a personality to match, he was the Mirador
resident she liked the least. She knew from some of the
things she'd overheard him say to Chris Morgan that he had
asked for some simulacra of his own—women like the one
behind the desk, only designed to function best in a
horizontal position.

The idea made her queasy, but at the same time she was
glad that Tom was leaving her alone. Apparently he had a

high sex drive, and he'd tried a couple of times to get something going with her. When she'd made it clear she wasn't interested, he'd pouted for a few days before thinking up his plan to have the hotel fulfill any fantasy. Of course he'd had to ask Art Landon to design the women for him. She wondered what *that* conversation had been like. Probably Landon had been embarrassed—but not Tom.

She went up to her room where she'd have some privacy—not in the absolute sense, but at least she'd be out of view of the other patients. A kind of electric anticipation coursed through her as she dressed in the casual running suit she'd woken up wearing the first time she'd found herself in the hotel. Knowing she was stalling, she finally lay down on her bed, keeping her breath even as she closed her eyes and tried to send her mind away from the virtual reality.

Mack had been a patient here and left this place, but he'd been able to use Lily's interface with the computer in the lab. Jenny couldn't do that because if she asked to use it, Lily would know that something was up. Plus, she might say it was the wrong time for Jenny to change her status.

But she had been thinking for days that she didn't need an interface—if her will was strong enough to do the trick.

As she lay on her bed, she tried a trick that she'd used several times. She slitted her eyes, staring at the familiar room, her gaze not quite in focus. Feeling her heart pound, she lowered her lids, and kept her eyes closed for almost a minute, trying to relax and also trying to project her consciousness into her body. She thought she felt a change, but waited a few more seconds before peering out from below her lashes. This time she saw another scene—the lab where her body was really sleeping in its special bed. Well, not sleeping, she supposed, if she was seeing the lab.

Lying very still, she looked around, past other beds toward a figure in a white coat at the far end of the room. It was Lily, checking computer readouts. Did she see something on Jenny's chart? As though to confirm the supposition, Lily turned, and Jenny closed her eyes quickly. She strained her ears, hearing Lily coming closer, then imagined her standing over her bed.

"Jenny?"

She didn't answer.

"Jenny, can you hear me? I thought I saw indications of consciousness in your brain waves."

Again she pretended that she was oblivious to the other woman.

Lily touched her hand. "Grant is hoping you'll wake up."

Her expression must have changed.

"You heard that, didn't you? You want to see Grant, don't you?"

She'd just seen Grant. And she wanted to see him now, but she couldn't afford that luxury.

Lily was speaking again. "I know you're near the surface. There's nothing to be afraid of. It's all right to wake up."

Nothing to be afraid of? If only that were true. Too many bad things had happened to her to believe in the fairy tale of safety.

Carlos did some research before he left the well-guarded compound where Rambo lived.

Using one of the private databases available to the staff, he called up a master list of medical workers in the Bethesda area. To his annoyance, there was no specific category for personnel who had worked at the Hamilton Lab. Taking another approach, he went to a job search board Hamilton had used when he'd been looking for a doctor who had worked with coma patients.

Several people had interviewed for the job, and Hamilton had hired a woman named Lily Wardman who had trained at Johns Hopkins.

She was the most senior staff member after Hamilton. Had she been the one to take over when the researcher's experiment were involuntarily terminated? Maybe, but he found no specific record of responsibility for the project being transferred to her. Yet he had to think someone had taken over. They wouldn't just abandon a bunch of half-dead patients, would they? Or maybe they would. That thought sent a chill up his spine, and he had to get up and go to his room where he poured some of the vodka he kept in a dresser drawer into a bathroom glass and took several gulps.

After stewing for a few minutes, he decided there was another way to approach the problem. What was Dr. Wardman doing now?

He went back to the computer, this time focusing on the doctor and not the project.

Dr. Wardman was currently working for an outfit called Decorah Security. Further digging revealed that they were a private detective agency. So what was a brain doctor doing for them?

He did more checking, but he couldn't find anything specific.

There was a nice Web page for Decorah Security. It was run by a guy named Frank Decorah, who advertised himself as an ex-Navy SEAL. And his agency had its main place of business in an office park in Beltsville, Maryland, near the USDA Agricultural Research Library, a much less prestigious location than Dr. Hamilton had chosen. It was like he'd deliberately decided to keep a low profile. There was no record of his running a lab experimenting on wigged-out patients. But that didn't mean he wasn't doing it. Or maybe he'd shifted from experiments to maintenance.

Next on Carlos's agenda would be to scout them out.

CHAPTER FIVE

Lily had planned to bring the new patient, Jonas Corker, into the VR in the morning. But she'd had some last minute details to attend to in his paperwork—and she wanted to have all her i's dotted and her t's crossed, unlike her previous boss who had gone to very questionable lengths to acquire subjects for his experiments.

It wasn't until the afternoon that she was actually ready to proceed with the introduction of Corker into the VR.

Assisted by her head orderly, Terry Montrose, she started with a thorough check of the patient's physical condition. He'd been working in a warehouse when a large crate had fallen off a high shelf and clipped him on the back of the skull. As a result, he'd suffered considerable brain damage, and the neurological staff at George Washington University Hospital had concluded there was no way he would ever wake up.

Because Lily had sent letters to various area hospitals explaining what Decorah was doing to help comatose patients, the chief of the GW neurology department, a Dr. Lawrence Young had called to say he might have a patient for her.

Corker was divorced with no family, which meant there was no one who could participate in his medical decisions.

She'd accepted the patient on the proviso that if he didn't work out in the VR, she could send him to a long-term care facility—which would mean he would be no better than a vegetable.

As she looked down at his slack face, she felt her heart squeeze. She'd gotten into this field because of her own sister, Shelly, who'd been previously warehoused as a hopeless case. But now she was in the VR and enjoying a new found lease on her life.

She could never leave, but that didn't matter to Shelly, and certainly not to Lily. She was just glad her sister was lucky enough to be living in a beautiful environment that provided care and stimulation. And she hoped it could be the same for Corker.

Turning her focus back to him, she said a little prayer for success. Right now he looked so vulnerable and helpless, but she knew from experience that the situation could change dramatically in the VR. And unlike Dr. Hamilton, she'd bring him in and explain the opportunity he'd been given.

Corker was already hooked up to the equipment that would send him into the artificial environment. While she was making the final preparations, she was aware of Mack standing behind her.

Turning, she gave him a reassuring look. "I've taken every precaution."

"But you could still get hurt."

"In the first place, we'll be in a virtual reality. In the second place, you'll be there to make sure I'm okay."

She could tell from his expression that he still didn't like the setup, but all he said was, "When are you sending him in?"

"As soon as Grant arrives," she answered, wanting to get it over with but at the same time a little reluctant to begin, now that the moment of truth had come. She knew from personal experience that this could go terribly wrong, and she had no way of predicting which patients were going to work out and which ones were too damaged to make the leap into the virtual world. Hopefully, she'd learn some way to find out—starting with her observations of this man. Or could she draw any general conclusions from him? It might turn out that each case was different.

Moments later, Grant walked in. "Ready?" he asked.

"Yes," Lily answered decisively.

Lying in her bed in the lab, Jenny Seville breathed out a small sigh of relief. From her eavesdropping, she'd known that Lily was planning to bring the new guy into the VR in the morning, and she'd lain among the other patients, her eyes slitted, watching the activity in the facility. Hooked up to the VR machinery, it had been hard to stay in the real world. She'd kept slipping back into the artificial environment against her will. Then she'd have to send her mind back to her own body all over again. Each time she'd thought she might have missed the transfer of the new patient, and each time nothing had happened with the new man.

Now finally, it looked like it was really going to happen. She tensed her muscles as she watched the preparations.

The staff were all busy with the new guy. Then she saw Terry Montrose start to check the other patients, and she drew in a quick breath. Was he going to screw this up for her?

She let herself drift back, away from the surface. Still she was aware of Montrose stopping to check the readouts on her bed. Apparently he was satisfied because he moved on after only a few minutes.

While Grant sat down at the desk with the VR monitor, Lily and Mack went into the dressing room and donned the standard medical gowns that the patients were wearing. Then she hooked Mack up to an IV line and put him under.

Watching the monitor over Grant's shoulder, she saw him wake up in the room she'd prepared off the hotel lobby in the Hotel Mirador. Involuntarily, she glanced back toward the bed in the lab where he was lying. It was always strange to see someone in two places—lying still and silent in a special hospital bed and animated in the artificial environment.

On the screen, he sat up, looked at the monitor and gave her and his brother a thumbs up. She waved back, then walked to Corker's bed. He was already hooked up to an IV line. All she had to do was send him into the room where Mack was waiting. He arrived on the sofa, still sleeping. And the way she'd set things up, he shouldn't awaken until she joined him and gave him a stimulant.

Still, she couldn't stop herself from feeling a small jolt of anxiety as she climbed into her own bed. She'd acted confident in front of Mack and Grant, but this was only the second time she'd brought anyone beyond the initial patient population into the VR. The first new inductee had been her sister, Shelly, who had been comatose since an auto accident when she was a child. But technically she'd been in the VR already, brought in by the hacker hired to find a criminal hiding there. That was the first time she'd been "awake" in years. Now she was living happily in the artificial environment, watched over by a nursemaid who was like the woman behind the desk—only designed with the attributes of a caring nursery school teacher.

"Ready?"

Grant's voice brought her back to the present.

"Yes." She looked over at Terry Montrose. As he stepped forward, ready to put her under, she closed her eyes and ordered herself to relax. When she opened them again, she was in the anteroom with Mack and Corker.

Jenny had tried to stay aware of what was going on in the patient facility. Hoping she wasn't jumping the gun, she opened her eyes fully, blinking in the light from the overhead fluorescents. Turning her head, she could see Grant hovering over the monitor across the room, watching the action in the VR anteroom. The orderly, Terry Montrose, was also facing the screen. Apparently this moment was too compelling for him to take his attention away from the induction process.

Jenny's heart was pounding now. She'd planned something like this for weeks, trying to think of all the angles. But here was her best chance, and she wasn't sure she could pull it off.

What if she failed? Would she be any worse off than she was now?

Could this totally backfire? Like could she kill herself—or set back her recovery for months? Those were legitimate questions, and logically she should have discussed them with Lily, her physician. But she'd been determined to keep Lily and everybody else out of the loop.

Before she could change her mind, she moved her hand, reaching up to detach the IV line hooked to her arm.

She pulled the connection out of the port and waited with her heart pounding. Long seconds passed, and she felt pretty normal, all things considered. Cautiously she pushed herself up and immediately felt light-headed. Easing back down, she waited for a few more minutes, then looked up again. She could see Grant and Terry still staring at the screen, their backs to her. All she could do was pray that they were they both caught up enough in the VR drama so she could get out of here without their being the wiser.

She rocked back and forth in the bed, getting used to the feel of her muscles working.

Praying she wasn't going to fall on her face and staying low, she swung her body over the side of the bed and eased down so that she was standing on the floor. It was a shock to feel the cold tiles under her bare feet, and she fought not to cry out. Instinctively, she clamped her hands on the rails and hung on.

She'd been horizontal for so long. Now she was seized by a wave of dizziness as though all the blood was rushing out of her head.

Glancing across the room, she saw the men were still focused on what was happening in the VR.

She wanted to get away before one of them turned around, but if she tried to move fast, she knew she would end up on her face. How much time did she have? There was no way of knowing.

Moving very quietly, she eased to the next bed, and saw Tom Wright lying there, his lips turned up in a grin.

It looked like he was having a good time in the imaginary world Art Landon had created. Turning her head away, she tried not to think about what he was probably doing.

Making sure Grant and Terry were still focused on the screen, she moved to the next bed—heading for the room where Mack and Lily had changed their clothes. There was no way to move quickly, and it seemed to take forever to reach the door. But finally she knew she was out of the men's sight if one of them happened to turn around. Of course, there was still the danger that Terry would make another sweep through the beds.

Hoping he was too absorbed in the drama unfolding in the VR, Jenny eased along the wall, still unsteady on her feet. She'd planned this escape, but she hadn't been absolutely sure she had the guts—or the stamina—to do what was necessary.

Breathing hard from the exertion, she sat down on the bench next to the clothes Lily had laid there. After stripping off her hospital gown with a shaky hand, she pulled Lily's knit top over her head, thankful that the doctor was about her size. Next she pulled on the woman's slacks and sat panting from the effort. Too bad everything she did seemed to take hours and drain her of energy. Now she understood that when she'd pictured herself walking out of the building, she hadn't been realistic. But she wasn't going to wimp out. Either she'd make it out of here, or she'd get caught.

By Grant? When she thought of the way he'd look when he discovered her escape attempt, she felt like the floor was falling away from under her. He'd be confused. Angry. And he'd feel betrayed. She was sure of that. So she'd better not let him catch her.

Unsteadily, she pulled on Lily's socks and shoes.

Finally dressed, she dragged in a breath and let it out. She had come this far, and she wasn't going to give up. But she was beginning to think she had to do a couple of things that were going to make her feel even worse than she did now.

Teeth gritted, she looked around the room and spotted a bank of lockers. After tottering over to them, she steadied herself with one hand while she opened doors with the other. She found the one Lily had used.

Before she could change her mind, she took out the other woman's purse. Rummaging inside she found her keys. She opened more lockers and found a set of men's clothes. Mack's she hoped.

Why was it better to steal from him than from Terry Montrose? she asked herself as she opened his wallet.

He had what looked like $250 in cash. Not a lot, but maybe enough.

If she hadn't been desperate, she might have been disgusted by her actions. She justified her behavior by telling herself that she was doing everyone a favor by disappearing because they didn't know what they'd gotten themselves into by accepting her as a patient.

Even if she stole from Mack and Lily, that was better than their getting shot by the men she was sure were looking for her.

She flipped open Lily's wallet and went very still as she stared at a picture of Grant with that crooked smile she had come to love.

No, not Grant, she reminded herself. It was Mack, his twin brother. It was tempting to take the picture anyway. A reminder of the man who had made love with her yesterday, the man she loved, she admitted as she felt her heart squeeze inside her chest.

But the picture wasn't Grant, and she left it in the plastic sleeve. Instead she slipped Lily's ID from her wallet and put it back in the purse, along with Mack's money. She left Lily's wallet on the bench. The ID and the purse were enough.

As she prepared to leave, she caught a glance at herself in the mirror near the door and went very still. In the VR she'd been the picture of vitality. The woman who stared back at her now looked pale and unhealthy, with deep circles under her eyes and hair that needed a good washing.

But what did she expect? She'd been lying in a modified hospital bed for months, shut away from the sun. She was just damn lucky that the bed was specially designed to keep her body in reasonable shape. If not, she would have gotten up and fallen flat on her face.

With a grimace, she tried to center herself, then looked out again at the men, who were still glued to the monitor—watching whatever compelling scene was playing out in the VR.

Hoping she was as invisible to them as a ghost, she slid along the wall, heading for the exit to the patient area.

CHAPTER SIX

In the VR, Lily looked from Corker to Mack and back again, giving herself a few minutes to get comfortable in the artificial setting.

Mack pressed his shoulder against hers. "You remember the first time we woke up here?"

She winced. "Yes, Hamilton sent me in here to lie to you— and all the other patients. And he didn't even give me a very convincing script. You knew there was something weird about me."

"That's not what I was thinking about."

"I know. But when I think about that first day, I feel ashamed."

"Your behavior wasn't your decision. You were obeying instructions from your superior not to reveal where we really were."

"Yes, And now he's gone, I'm running the show, and I'm going to be up front with Jonas Corker."

Getting up, she went to the desk, opened a side drawer, and took out a hypodermic. It seemed like a strange thing to do in a virtual environment, yet after reevaluating the needs of the patients and also any staff who went inside, she'd created some safeguards. They'd set the place up to be as real as possible. And that meant having a way to wake up patients in the artificial environment and sedate them if necessary.

After checking the label on the hypodermic, she crossed the room, knelt by Corker and gave him an injection in the forearm.

Tension sizzled through her as she waited for what would happen next.

"Is something wrong?" Mack whispered.

"I hope not. I haven't done this before, and it could take a little while," she added.

As she watched, Corker's facial muscles twitched. Then his eyelids fluttered. After several more seconds his eyes snapped open. At first his vision looked like it was directed inward. Then he focused on her as though trying to figure out if he had seen her before.

His lips moved, but no sound came out.

When he turned his head away, she put her hand on his shoulder, and he jumped like someone had touched him with a hot poker.

Quickly she pulled her hand back. "Jonas."

His head twisted back toward her, his expression wary. "Do I know you?"

"No. We just met. I'm Lily Wardman," she answered. She could have said, "Dr. Wardman," but she'd made the split-second decision not to make him worry about that immediately. So much for full disclosure.

"Where am I?" he asked in a thick voice, his eyes darting around the small room, then back to her.

"Somewhere safe."

He looked like he didn't believe her.

As she gave him a little more space, he made a moaning sound. "The boxes. I saw the boxes falling. I felt ..." His voice trailed off.

"It's okay. You're safe," she repeated.

"I don't think so."

He pushed himself up, keeping his gaze on her as though he was prepared for some kind of unexpected—and dangerous—move on her part. When she stayed still, trying to project a nonthreatening aura, his focus shifted to Mack.

"Who are you?"

"I'm Mack Bradley."

"Are you a security guard?"

Mack looked to Lily, and she gave an almost imperceptible shake of her head.

"I'm Lily's husband," he said.

"Oh yeah. Well I can tell from your expressions there's something fishy going on. What are you hiding?"

"Nothing. You need to know what happened and where you are now."

"I know where I'm am," Corker shot back. "I'm in hell, and you're trying to get me to relax so you can torture me."

"No. Of course not."

"I'm dead."

"No."

Ignoring her reassurance, he plowed on, "I know all those heavy boxes hit me. And you can't fool me. I know where I ended up."

"You're not dead, and you're not in hell," Lily said in a voice that she hoped was reassuring.

Corker sat up, glancing around the small room as though he was looking for an escape route.

"We're here to help you," Lily said, glad that she had thought to prepare this room, "You were injured, and you're ... better."

"You're lying."

At that moment, the door flew open, and Shelly burst into what was supposed to be a private encounter. The little girl had a gleeful expression on her face as she ran toward Lily.

"See, Anna was right. You're here. She told me you were here."

Lily felt her face go rigid with shock. Obviously the computer program knew that she was coming with a new patient, but she hadn't expected her sister to find out about it and rush to see her. Behind her, she could see Anna, the simulated nursemaid who kept the rambunctious child from getting into too much trouble.

Before Lily could react, the man on the couch leaped up. "Demon," he shouted as he launched himself at the little girl.

"No," Lily screamed as she leaped into his path, trying to block him.

Mack jumped up as well, putting himself between Lily, Shelly and the maddened patient. The guy came out swinging and hit him in the chest.

Trying to keep from getting socked in the jaw, Mack shoved the guy away. He bounced back, colliding with Lily, who came down hard on the floor, banging her back painfully against the edge of the sofa. For long moments, she lay stunned.

The scene of chaos gave the new patient an opening. Pushing himself up, he shoved Mack out of the way and made for the door again. The frantic series of attacks and responses might have been a scene from an action comedy movie, except that none of it was funny.

"Anna, take Shelly out of here," Lily cried out as Mack grabbed for Corker.

In the lab, Jenny heard Grant make a startled sound. Something was happening, but she couldn't see what it was because Terry Montrose had crowded in closer, their bodies blocking her view of the monitor.

Obviously things weren't going the way anybody had expected.

"Mack, what do you need?" Grant called out.

Jenny didn't stay to hear the answer. Thinking that she couldn't have arranged things better if she'd tried, she slipped along the wall, then out into the reception area.

She felt a pang of worry—and guilt. Lily and Mack must be in trouble, but it was only in the VR, she reminded herself. Nothing permanent could happen to them there, could it?

From what Lily had told the patients, Jenny knew Dr. Hamilton's original lab was in a fancy office building in Bethesda. Grant had said they'd been moved to a much more modest facility in an industrial park between Baltimore and Washington.

The lobby was pretty small. She stuck close to the wall, using it to keep herself steady as she approached a security desk.

To her relief, it was unmanned, because security was lighter here than at Hamilton's facility. Mack had gone into the VR with Lily, and Grant had stationed himself where he could monitor the situation. Now they were both busy with whatever emergency Lily had encountered when she'd tried to introduce the new guy into the Mirador environment.

That knowledge brought another pang of guilt. Since they were running a minimal operation unknown to the public, they thought they didn't need a lot of protection. But they didn't know that some very bad men were looking for Jenny Seville. Well, not Seville, she reminded herself. That wasn't her real name. And she was praying that would keep them from figuring out where she was.

She took a deep breath, wavering on her feet as she bent over the desk and started opening drawers. Grant had told her they kept weapons here as a precaution, and she found an automatic pistol in the top middle drawer. Taking it was another reason to feel guilty, but she did it anyway.

She checked the action, put the gun into Lily's purse, and headed for the door. Outside she found herself facing a narrow parking lot, backed by ugly one-story cinder-block buildings, with a strip of grass along the margin. After the blue skies of the Mirador Hotel, it was startling to see gray clouds hiding the sun. And after the sparking clean grounds of the hotel, the warehouse area looked grubby.

The heat was another shock to her system. At the Mirador, the temperature was always a pleasant seventy degrees. Now the full force of a Maryland summer enveloped her. It was like stepping into an overused laundry room, and she struggled to draw in a full breath of air.

The change of scene was a shock, but this was the real world, where she'd have to function now. And she'd taken a lot of chances getting to this point.

She didn't know which car was Mack and Lily's, but she pressed the unlock button on the ignition key and heard a chirp. Pressing several more times, she followed the sound to a newish-looking Honda.

After clicking once more, she opened the door and slipped into the fiery interior. When she leaned back against the headrest, the hot seat cover burned her neck, and she hunched forward, taking several deep breaths of the overheated air. She was amazed that she had gotten this far, but it wasn't far enough. At any moment, Grant could come charging out of the building shouting at her to come back.

Knowing she had to get away, she turned the ignition, hoping the air conditioning was going to cool the car soon. She had to get away from the lab and find somewhere to hole up. But how far could she go in this condition?

After wiping sweat from her forehead with the back of her arm, she glanced toward the building, but apparently nobody had discovered her absence yet. Taking a chance on staying a little longer, she clicked on the GPS. It displayed a map of the area, and she saw that the industrial park was off a major north-south highway—Route 1. There ought to be convenient motels out there, but she'd better not pick the first one she came to.

She closed her eyes for a moment, praying that she had the strength to do this—and that she wasn't going to die of heatstroke before the AC kicked in. Then she backed cautiously out of the parking space.

To Lily's dismay, Corker made it out of the door and into the lobby. Apparently the large, luxurious space was not what he was expecting. He stopped short and cried out in surprise, giving Mack the opportunity to catch and push him down to the marble floor.

The man had been unconscious for several weeks, and although his status had changed in the VR, he was in no shape to fight a guy who worked out regularly in the real world.

"Lily, can you get a hypo?" Mack shouted.

"I'm coming. Hold him."

As she spoke, Lily crawled to the table next to the couch and fumbled in the drawer. When she found the other hypodermic, she pushed herself up, stumbled into the lobby and jammed the needle into his arm. For a terrifying half minute, he continued to struggle against Mack. Then he suddenly went slack, and Mack grabbed him by the shoulders, pulled him into the greeting room, and eased him to the sofa, where he lay sprawled.

"Thanks," Lily said.

"I guess he's not in as good mental shape as you thought. You should ship him to that facility you have in reserve."

"We may have to," Lily said as she crossed the room and hurried into the hotel lobby.

She saw Paula Rendell and Anna crouched on either side of Shelly who was sobbing, tears running down her cheeks.

Lily ran to her sister, knelt down and reached for the little girl who came into her arms, still crying.

"I didn't do anything to that man, but he wanted to hurt me," Shelly sobbed.

"No. He was scared of you."

"Why?"

"He's confused. But it's okay. I put him to sleep. Everything's okay," Lily soothed as she gathered her little sister close, stroking her back. Shelly's auto accident had been when she was eight. That was more than twenty years ago, but the girl's mental development had been arrested at that age. She would never mature. She would always react like a child. And though her body had become a woman's in the real world, in the VR she still looked like the youngster she had been when she was injured.

Overcome with guilt for having put her sister in danger, Lily rocked the little girl in her arms. "It's okay, sweetheart."

"That man scared me."

"I know. But he can't hurt you now. Uncle Mack and I put him to sleep," she repeated what she'd said.

Gradually, Shelly's crying subsided. She looked up at Lily, her expression troubled. "I didn't know I shouldn't go in there."

"Yes. It was a mistake for me not to tell Anna. But it's okay."

"Why was he so mad?"

"He was afraid. And he reacted by getting mad."

Shelly bobbed her head.

Over her shoulder, Lily regarded Anna who looked like she wished she could sink into the floor. "I didn't know that was wrong," she said.

"It's not your fault," Lily answered, feeling a little strange reassuring a woman who was only part of an elaborate computer program. "Next time we'll make sure you know we need privacy."

"You were bringing in a new patient?" Paula asked.

"Yes."

The travel agent kept her gaze on Lily. "And it didn't go so well."

"Unfortunately."

"So he's not coming in after all?"

"I'm not giving up so quickly," Lily answered.

Mack, who had been standing back while she comforted her sister made a rough sound. "Oh please. He's a menace."

"I don't want to just give up on him," she repeated. "I'd like to try again after using a tranquilizer. If I can convince him he's not in hell ..."

"Yeah, and you have to wonder why he thought he should go there. I mean what did he do in life that was so bad?"

"It could have been something very minor—if he belonged to a strict religious sect. Or his parents could have drummed the concept of sin into him."

Mack made a snorting sound. He looked like he wanted to argue. Instead, he pressed his lips together.

"He was scary," Shelly said.

"I would never let him hurt you," Lily said, then looked at Anna. "Why don't you take Shelly down to the ice cream parlor?"

When Art had designed the Mirador, he had copied a hotel he had visited in India. The luxury location had been a nice starting point, but since the patients had arrived, they and Lily had made suggestions for additions to improve the environs where they were confined.

The Ice Cream Shop was one of Lily's suggestions.

"Can you come, too?" Shelly asked, a pleading tone in her voice. "I thought I was gonna get to hang out with you when I heard you were coming to the hotel."

Lily debated. There was nothing she could do for Corker at the moment, and maybe spending a little time with her sister after the traumatic incident was a good idea.

She glanced at Mack. "We can take a few minutes, I think."

"Okay."

The whole group headed to the other side of the lobby, then out onto one of the covered colonnades that were a feature of the hotel architecture. In the heat of the actual Indian environment they would have provided needed shade. At the Mirador they were purely decorative.

The adults strolled along. Shelly skipped beside them, obviously feeling a lot better than when she'd come into the arrival room.

As they drew near the ice cream parlor, Shelly reached for Lily's hand.

"You're not mad at me, are you?" she asked.

Lily looked down at the little girl. "Of course not."

"But I wasn't supposed to go into that room."

"It wasn't your fault."

They reached the Ice Cream Shop, which was patterned after pictures Lily has seen in an old magazine from the fifties. It had chairs with bent-wire backs, round tables with marble tops, and a black and white patterned floor. White lattice panels decorated the walls.

A young man behind the counter snapped to attention as they came in. He was another one of the staff who had been added to the program.

"Help you?" he asked.

"What flavors do you have?" Paula asked.

"This week we have chocolate, vanilla, strawberry, chocolate chip ..."

"Do you have the mocha almond I asked for?" Paula interrupted.

"Yes."

Shelly got her usual—chocolate chip with various toppings. Paula got her request. Lily chose strawberry, and Mack asked for his usual chocolate. It amused Lily to note that Anna copied Shelly's choice. Although the simulacrum couldn't taste the treat, she did a nice job of appearing to enjoy herself.

Recovered from her earlier shock, Shelly chattered about the fun things she'd been doing. Although Lily tried to relax, she was having trouble concentrating. She was still thinking about Corker and what she could do to help him.

Was his brain too damaged to function here? Was there some way to ease him into the environment? Could she arrange therapy sessions for him? And why, exactly, did he think he'd ended up in hell? She'd studied his background and thought he was okay, but perhaps he'd done some clandestine things that made him dangerous to the other patients here.

Everybody was down to the last quarter of their ice cream when Lily's phone vibrated.

She saw from the screen that the call was from Terry Montrose.

Excusing herself, she stepped into the colonnade.

As soon as she clicked the phone button, Terry's voice came through low and urgent.

"Lily, I'm afraid we've got a problem."

CHAPTER SEVEN

"What's wrong?" Lily asked.

"Jenny Seville is missing."

"What? Did I hear that right?"

Mack had come out and was standing close enough to Lily to hear Terry say, "Jenny Seville isn't in her bed."

"That's impossible."

"She's not there."

"We'll be right over." Lily darted back into the ice cream parlor, stopping short when she saw the alarm on Shelly's face.

"Something bad happened," the little girl said.

"Nothing to do with you. It's about the place where I work. I have to go back now, but you can finish your ice cream with Anna and Paula."

"When will you be back?"

"I'm not sure, but soon."

Mack was waiting for her outside, and they hurried back to the main part of the hotel. On the way, she called Terry. "Bring Corker back to his bed. We'll come through the dedicated interface."

Upstairs in her bedroom, she stepped into the portal that they could use as a passage between the VR and the lab.

Moments after setting the controls, she was back in her bed and sitting up.

55

And Mack wasn't far behind her.

The moment Lily came back to her body, she felt a throbbing headache.

Ignoring it, she detached the medical gear and lowered herself to the floor. Mack did the same.

"Where have you looked?" she asked Terry, who was standing beside her bed, his expression apologetic.

"I ... I was afraid to leave the other patients. Grant is searching the building."

"Okay." She wanted to rail at the man, but she didn't see any point in blaming this on him. All of them had been focused on Corker. And none of them had been paying any attention to Jenny or the other patients.

But now that Lily reflected on it, she realized the young woman had been behaving oddly for some time. Lily had noted she was close to waking up, and she'd assumed the young woman was afraid to rejoin the real world. Apparently it was just the opposite. She'd been planning to rejoin the world—on her own terms.

And the crisis with Corker had given her the perfect opportunity.

"I'm so sorry," Terry said.

"We all are," Lily answered before she and Mack headed for the locker room to get dressed. When she stepped inside, she stopped short.

"What?" Mack asked.

"My clothes are missing."

"Jesus."

"She must have taken them. I think we can be sure she was planning this for a while." She went to the supply shelves and took down a pair of scrub pants and a shirt, which she pulled on. When she opened her locker, she got another shock.

Mack was in the process of pulling on his shirt when he heard her gasp.

"What?"

"My purse is missing."

"Christ."

Grant strode into the dressing room but stopped when he saw that Lily was still securing the waistband of the pants. "Sorry."

"I'm decent," she answered. "Did you search the building?"

He looked sick when he said, "She's definitely gone. And your car is missing." He muttered a curse. "And so is a gun from the security desk out front."

The three of them looked at each other.

Grant made an angry sound. "I knew she was worried about something."

"All along it seemed like she was hiding out in the VR," Mack said. "When we all woke up there the first time, she didn't even want to tell us her name."

"Yeah," Grant muttered. "She was using the VR for a bolt-hole. Then she must have decided it wasn't safe to stay. I guess that's why she wanted all that self-defense training." He ran a shaky hand through his hair. "I wanted to help her, dammit. But I just couldn't get her to open up."

"This isn't your fault. She obviously had her own agenda."

"I should have made her come clean with me." His face hardened. "When I find her I'm going to ..." He let the end of the sentence dangle because too many emotions were raging inside him. Really, he didn't know what he was going to do. All he knew was that he was angry with himself for trusting her. Angry with himself for being half in love with her. And angry about what she had just done.

"I guess we'd better assume she had her reasons. I mean, I think it was an act of desperation," Mack said, obviously trying to take Grant's anger down a notch.

He answered with a tight nod.

Switching to the immediate problem, Grant added, "She might have taken the car, but let's assume she's in no shape to drive far, and she's smart enough to realize it. We're right on a major north-south route, with plenty of motels. I'm betting she's in one of them."

"She could take any side street," Grant said.

"She could," Mack acknowledged. "But she doesn't know the area. And she can't be feeling great. I remember how I functioned when I came out of the VR for the first time after being in there for a month. I'm guessing she's only going far enough to think she's safe before getting a room."

Grant sighed. "Okay, you go south, and I can go north." He turned to Lily, a stark expression on his face. "How much money was in your wallet?"

"She left my money and took Mack's"

Grant turned to his brother. "How much?"

"I'm not sure. Around two hundred dollars. Why?"

"I'm trying to judge what kind of room she'd get."

"You think she's savvy enough not to use Lily's credit cards?" Mack shot back.

Grant shrugged. "I suppose it depends on how many thriller novels she's read."

Mack made an impatient gesture. "Okay we're wasting time. We'd better get the show on the road. We'll keep in touch, so each of us knows what the other is doing."

When he said, "keep in touch," he wasn't talking about using their cell phones. He was referring to the ability he had with his twin brother to communicate mentally. They'd had it as boys, lost it as teens, and gotten it back when Mack was in the VR and Grant was in the real world searching for him.

"And I'll call Frank," Lily said, looking miserable about having to report the screwup.

Mack started for the door, then stopped and cursed.

"What?" Grant asked.

"Lily and I came in the same car."

"You can use mine," Terry said from the main room. "It's my fault she's gone," he added, sounding like a guy on his way to the electric chair. "I should have checked the patients periodically."

"No," Grant corrected. "Both of us were watching the action on the screen. She knew it, and she took advantage of the situation. And when Corker went batshit, that gave her even more time to slip away without our noticing."

"And I should have gotten an extra staffer in here," Lily added. "But who would have thought Jenny was looking for an opportunity to bolt?" She spread her hands. "There's no point in our beating ourselves up for what we should have done."

Grant answered with a nod, but he was already thinking about current strategy. "Probably there's no point in stopping at the first few motels," he said as he and his brother headed for the door.

"But I guess we have to do it anyway, in case she suddenly realized she would be a fool to drive far. Or she stayed close like a double fake out," Mack countered.

In the parking lot, they headed for separate cars. As soon as Grant was inside, he sent a message to his brother. *Can you hear me?*

The answer came back almost at once, *Yeah.*

When they'd first rediscovered the ability to talk mind to mind, they had only been able to communicate over short distances. But they had been practicing the skill, and now they had a range of several miles. Too bad they hadn't checked the limit of their power. But there had been no need for long-distance communication until now.

Grant pulled out of the parking lot first and turned right. Mack was behind him and turned left.

He had tried to keep his attention focused on the immediate task. Now that he was alone, it was impossible to hold his emotions at bay.

He hated to admit that he'd been falling in love with Jenny Seville. He'd thought her feelings were similar. Otherwise why would she have finally gone to bed with him after all these months? But was he attributing too much to a few hours in a cabana by the pool at the Mirador Hotel?

Afterwards she'd reverted to her closed-up self. Because she didn't trust him? Because she was afraid to get involved with him? Or because she thought she was a danger to him and everyone in the VR?

He sighed. Without more input from her, it had been impossible to figure out why she wouldn't level with him. And now what was he going to do when he found her. Hug her in relief that he'd caught up with her or try and shake the truth out of her?

Maybe it would be better if Mack was the one who located her. That might give Grant time to cool off.

Up ahead was a medium-priced national chain. He slowed and pulled into the parking lot, then stopped under the covered entrance and sat for a minute. They'd rushed out of the Decorah facility so fast that he hadn't thought about his approach.

At that moment, Mack contacted him, and he was glad of the distraction.

I'm coming up on a Holiday Inn express. How are we going to work this?

Well, I was thinking I'd ask if Lily Wardman had registered, since that's the ID she has, and she probably looks enough like Lily to get away with it.

The hair color's wrong.

Women change their hair color all the time.

True. If they don't have Lily Wardman registered, we can describe her.

And why are we looking for her? Mack asked.

Grant thought about it. The reason had to be urgent, but he didn't want to say Jenny was a fugitive from the law—or an escaped mental patient. *How about, she has a serious medical condition and needs to report back to the hospital.*

What hospital?

The Decorah In-Patient Treatment Center. If they need confirmation they can call Lily.

Okay, Mack agreed. *I'll phone Lily and tell her she might be getting calls from desk clerks wanting to make sure they're not talking to an abusive husband.*

With the procedure worked out, Grant went into the motel and strode purposefully toward the desk.

A short, dark-haired man standing behind the desk looked up. His plastic name tag said Chuck. "Can I help you?"

"I hope so. I'm looking for a woman who might have come here during the past ..." He stopped and looked at his watch. "Past hour and a half."

It was hard to believe that so much had happened in such a short time, but there it was. Introducing Jonas Corker into the VR had looked like a catastrophe. It had been a snap to contain, compared to this.

When the clerk waited for Grant to go on, he said, "She was a patient in a hospital facility, and she has a life-threatening condition."

"Then why did she leave?" Chuck asked.

Grant kept his gaze steady. "She didn't want to acknowledge the seriousness of her illness."

"Which is what?"

"That's confidential medical information. But I can say that time is of the essence. Could you check to see if she's registered?"

"I'd want some confirmation from her doctor," the clerk said.

Grant dragged in a breath, realizing that he had a problem he hadn't even thought about. "She took her doctor's identification."

"Oh yeah?"

"When you call the hospital, Dr. Wardman will answer. She's standing by."

The guy gave Grant a long look, like he was trying to decide if all this was for real. When he shook his head, Grant was sure he was going to tell him to get the hell out. Instead he dialed the Decorah facility, and Grant could tell he was talking to Lily.

She must have answered and made the case sound urgent because the man hung up and turned to his computer. After checking his records, he shook his head again. "Not here under that name."

Still, Grant pressed on. He gave a description, including that the patient would probably have looked sick and shaky.

"No. I've been on duty for the past three hours, and I haven't seen anyone like you're talking about."

"Okay."

Chuck hesitated for a moment before asking, "Are you looking for her because she has a mental problem."

"No."

"She's physically sick?"

"She was in a coma until recently," Grant answered evenly before turning on his heel. As soon as he'd said it, he wished he'd thought of a different answer, because that was a clue someone else could follow.

Back in the car, he dialed Lily.

"Was she there?" his sister-in-law asked anxiously

"No. This is the first place I tried. But we've got a screwy problem. The clerk wanted to call the hospital to confirm that a patient with a medical problem had left.

"And I did."

"But she took your ID."

"I wasn't thinking about that."

"Neither was I until I had to give your name."

"I can be Doctor Bradley."

"That will work, if I don't have to give *my* name. Then we're back to weird again.

"Well, let's try Dr. Bradley. Technically that's still me, although it's not my professional name. But it's not like the

Hamilton Lab. This facility is owned by Decorah Security, not me."

"Right."

He could hear a phone ringing now.

"That's Mack," she said.

"Can you make it a three way?"

"Yes."

As they spoke, he drove out of the motel lot and continued down Route 1 to the next chain motel. By the time he reached it, Mack had agreed to also use the name Dr. Bradley for the patient's doctor. And the brothers had refined their technique. If the next motel clerks asked, they would say the patient had a tropical infection that was not contagious but it was life threatening.

The results at Grant's next three motels were similarly frustrating. Lily Wardman had not registered. And he knew from his mental conversations with Mack that his brother was having similar luck.

Had he been wrong in his assessment?

By some force of will, had Jenny kept driving out of the area? And she was in Delaware by now, in some off-brand fleabag where nobody would think to look? If she'd gotten that far, there was little hope of finding her. But he didn't think she'd pick a fleabag to stay in. He'd known from her reaction to the Mirador that she was used to luxury, and she probably wouldn't want to stay in a place where there might be actual bugs.

He pressed doggedly on, prepared for another disappointment when he drove into the next place, another two-story chain, offering a free breakfast along with a room.

This time the clerk was a woman in her twenties who was reading a book at the counter. She quickly put it away when he came through the door. His spiel was well rehearsed now when he said, "I'm looking for a woman who might have gotten a room a couple of hours ago. She was in the hospital but checked herself out against medical advice. Her name is

Lily Wardman. She's in her twenties. Short caramel-colored hair and light eyes."

To his surprise, the clerk said, "Yes, she did check in. I thought she looked sick, and I gave her a room around back on the first floor. Room 152."

At first Grant could hardly believe what he was hearing. But as he absorbed the news, he felt a flood of relief—coupled with a stab of dread. This was what he had been hoping for, and at the same time, the knowledge that he was going to come face to face with Jenny again made his heart skip a beat, then start up in double time.

"Don't tell her I'm coming. I don't want her trying to run out on us again."

"Of course not."

He hurried back to his car, trying to picture the coming confrontation. He had half expected that Jenny would be impossible to find, and now she was only a few yards away—unless she'd changed her mind and skipped out of the motel.

That worry had him gunning the engine as he headed for the back of the two-story building. But he had to slow to read the room numbers.

As he drove along the row of parking spaces, he was relieved to see Mack's car sitting in front of room 152. He continued past and parked several slots away so she wouldn't know that the car outside had anything to do with her.

Walking back quietly, he kept his gaze fixed on 152. He could see that the curtains were drawn, with a thin line of light showing at the sides.

Now that he was here, another thought occurred to him and almost choked off his breath.

What if Jenny had escaped the VR so she could meet someone from outside? A friend? A lover? A partner in crime. Up till now, he hadn't considered that scenario, but anything could be possible.

He pressed his ear to the door, hearing nothing. But she'd left the light on, which he assumed meant she wasn't sleeping. Or had she passed out? Again his heart started to pound.

Hoping for the best but prepared for something he hadn't anticipated, he knocked on the door.

There was no answer.

With his pulse thrumming, he tried again.

"Who's there?" a woman's voice called out. Through the thick door, he thought it was Jenny, but he couldn't be sure.

"This is the front desk."

"What do you want?"

"You dropped your credit card in the lobby, miss." As soon as he said it, he wished he'd thought of something else. If she was smart, she hadn't even pulled out a credit card.

Long seconds passed before he heard footsteps. He moved to the side so that if she could see him at all in the peephole, his image would be so distorted that she couldn't tell who he was.

The light at the small opening changed, telling him that Jenny was looking out. Then she flung the door open. Framed in the lighted rectangle, she was holding a gun, pointed at Grant's chest.

CHAPTER EIGHT

Grant went very still, his mouth suddenly dry as old newspaper. He had worked with Jenny on weapons training. He knew she was a good shot. And there wasn't much chance of missing at this distance. On the other hand, a gunshot was sure to bring people running.

"Let me help you out," he said, trying to project iron calm. "If you're going to shoot me, it's probably better to do it behind a closed door so the cops don't come running."

Raising his hands palms out, he took a step forward, acting like he was perfectly sure she wouldn't drill him.

She could have said, "Don't come any closer. Instead, she grimaced and took a step back.

He moved a foot nearer—into the room, closing the door behind him with his shoulder.

"Do you really want to shoot me?" he asked.

"No."

"Then put the gun down."

After considering the suggestion, she laid the weapon on the combination dressing table, TV stand, and desk across from the bed, then sat down in the desk chair.

He'd been focused on the small hole in the barrel of the automatic. With the threat less immediate, he took a good look at the woman. Her shoulders were slumped. Her face was flushed, and she had dark circles under her eyes. "You look like hell," he said.

"I feel like hell."

"You should let Lily check you over."

"I left for a reason." She dragged in a breath and exhaled. "And she probably doesn't want to see me. I mean, you know I stole her purse and car, right? And Mack's money," she added to be perfectly clear about her sins.

The way she had said it tore at him. He had come here not sure whether he was angry or terrified for her safety. He still wasn't quite sure which impulse was stronger, but he crossed to where she sat, and lifted her into his arms, then carried her to the bed. Easing down, he stretched out, taking her with him so that the length of her body rested against his.

She could have resisted. Instead she buried her head against his shoulder, and he could feel her start to shake. Then she was sobbing.

He gathered her close, cradling her in his arms, closing his eyes while he hung on to her, feeling the waves of misery roll off of her.

He had been angry with her for disappearing. He was still angry, but now he knew how much he cared about her.

Finally, he felt her struggling to get control of herself. He eased away, went into the bathroom and came back with several tissues.

When she had wiped her eyes and blown her nose, he settled down beside her again.

He had forgotten all about his brother, when he heard Mack speak to him in his head.

Grant?

Yes.

Anything new to report?

Actually, yeah, I found her at the next place. You can go back to the lab.

Thank God. You're bringing her back?

I think so. She's pretty upset right now.

Okay. I'll leave you to it.

The conversation cut off and Jenny asked, "Where were you?"

"Talking to Mack."

She looked around, confused.

"Remember, I told you, he and I can speak mind to mind? We were both looking for you and keeping in communication. He went one way down Route 1 and I went the other. He, um 'called' to ask how the search was going. I told him I found you."

"So he's going back to the lab to tell the others?"

"Yes. Everybody was worried."

She gave a small nod.

They had finally come to the moment of truth.

"Maybe this is the time to tell me why you were so determined to train yourself for self-defense and why you were so desperate to leave."

Long seconds passed before she said, "I knew I was putting everyone in the VR and at the Decorah facility in danger."

"Why?"

Again she hesitated.

"I can't help you unless you trust me." He fixed her with a hard look. "And don't you think you have some kind of moral obligation to me and the others? Frank Decorah could have shipped all of Hamilton's patients to long-term care facilities. But he took over the obligation. And Lily stayed on to run the new facility. After Hamilton was arrested, they provided you with an environment where you could live."

"I wasn't thinking about it that way."

"Well, think about it now."

In a barely audible voice, she said, "I left because bad men are looking for me."

"Why?"

68

"Because they kidnapped me, and I escaped. I mean it was a close thing. I was lucky they'd let me out for some exercise, and I could hit my guard with a flower pot and steal the keys to a car."

"Kidnapped!"

"Yes"

"Then your family's looking for you? Did they call the police?"

She sighed. "My parents are both dead."

"What happened?"

"An auto accident," she said in a flat voice.

"Like you."

"Uh huh."

Was she telling the truth? He couldn't help wondering about that.

"Okay. So who kidnapped you?"

She closed her eyes, then opened them again. "You were right. I came from a very privileged background. I grew up on a big estate and went to an exclusive girls' school. My parents left me a big house and a lot of money. After they died, I went to college and got a degree. Then I got a teaching job. I met a man. The father of one of my students. It turned out he wasn't as nice as he pretended."

"In what way?"

"He wanted a relationship." She swallowed hard. "When I said, 'no,' he took me to his house and wouldn't let me leave."

Mack had spoken to his brother from the parking lot of a chain motel a few miles south of the Decorah facility on Route 1.

He hit the auto dial button on his cell phone and called Lily. She answered in a breathy voice.

"Mack, did you find her?"

"Grant did."

"Thank God," she said, echoing his reaction when he'd gotten the news from Grant. "Is everything okay?"

"I guess she didn't shoot him with the gun she stole."

Lily winced. "And he's bringing her back here?"

"I think so."

"She never should have left. She needs me to check her over."

"He's talking to her now, trying to find out why she ran."

"So you don't know anything—except that she's safe?"

"Yeah. He couldn't really talk. I'm on my way back. Do you want me to get anything from the grocery store?" he added.

It was a mundane request, but now that the emergency was over, life would go on as usual. Well, not quit usual. Lily was still worried about Corker and worried about Jenny's medical condition.

She thought for a moment. "It's been a heck of a day. Unless you want scrambled eggs for dinner, maybe we should just stop for takeout on the way home."

"Good idea. Pizza okay?" he asked, figuring he was due a reward for the night's activities.

"Sure. After I check Jenny over," she answered.

He grinned, glad that Dr. Wardman wasn't insisting on a healthy dinner.

He was still a couple of miles from the industrial park where the Decorah medical facility was located. He kept driving down the highway, reached the entrance to the park and turned in. The road leading into the complex was dark because most of the buildings were only in use during business hours, unlike Decorah which had to operate twenty-four seven.

His mind was on what kind of pizza to suggest for dinner when he snapped back to the scene around him. Several hundred yards down the road, at the entrance to the Decorah building, he saw something he wasn't expecting.

A dark-colored SUV had pulled up near the door. As he watched, three men got out. He didn't know how an ordinary citizen would react, but in the split second when he first spotted the group, he could see that they were carrying assault rifles.

He had been driving slowly on the narrow lane. Hitting the brake, he quickly pulled in to a parking space in front of another building and cut his lights. Drawing the automatic pistol from the holster under his jacket, he got out of the car and walked to a storefront called DSR. He stepped into the entryway, waiting with his heart thumping for the men to come down the sidewalk toward him. After half a minute, he breathed out a small sigh. Apparently he'd convinced the guys with the rifles that he hadn't seen the guns and that his business was elsewhere.

Christ, now what? He had a couple of options. It was probably too late to call Lily on the phone. Maybe his best bet was to call the main Decorah Security number.

Was Jenny telling the truth? It was a pretty unusual story, but it could be true. Or mostly true?

"What kind of man would do that?" Grant pressed.

"I guess you'd call him a gangster."

"The parent of one of your students?"

"Gangsters have children, too."

He watched Jenny swallow hard as her gaze turned inward. "Don't make me talk about it now. He had guards watching me. But I slipped away and got the keys to a car. I was trying to outrun them. I took a turn too fast—and you know the rest. Well, most of it. I guess Dr. Hamilton was on the lookout for subjects for his experiment, and he heard about a woman in the hospital with no name and no insurance. I guess he was thrilled to get me."

Grant was trying to digest all that when she said, "The safest thing for everyone at Decorah Security is for me to disappear."

"That's our call, not yours."

When she started to protest, he hurried on. "We need to go back and sort this out. And I'm sure Lily is going to want to give you an exam—and maybe put you back in bed. You had no business taking off like that."

"I thought that was best for everyone."

"No." He kept his gaze steady. "Did you think it was best for me? For us?"

She appeared to be fighting tears again. "I put you in danger."

"I'm trained to handle danger. So are the other Decorah agents."

She looked like she wanted to argue with him. Instead she switched the subject and murmured, "I'm going to feel awful when I see Lily. I mean, I stole from her."

"We'll sort it out," he repeated. Or would they? He couldn't help thinking that she still wasn't telling him everything. What did she still need to hide?

To his horror, he blurted the thing that was at the top of his mind. "Did the guy rape you?"

The suddenly sick expression on her face made him think he was right. And maybe that was the element he'd been missing. An experience like that could make a woman act in ways that weren't normal for her. It could also make her wary of intimacy. She'd taken a long time to get physical with him. That could be the reason. And it might be a good reason not to press her now. He'd come looking for her weighed down by a bundle of assumptions. Maybe he had to rethink everything he thought he knew.

* * *

Mack put the gun away and pulled out his phone, ready to call in more Decorah agents. Before he could dial, one of the men he'd seen stepped into his line of sight.

"Drop the phone. Hands in the air."

Shit. He'd thought he'd fooled them by ducking into the DSR doorway. Apparently they weren't taking any chances.

"Drop the phone. Hands in the air," the guy repeated, "If you don't want a nice neat hole in the middle of your forehead."

Would the guy do it? Mack knew that the industrial park was almost deserted at this hour. But the guy might not know that, and he might not want to advertise his presence with a shot. Still, Mack wasn't going to bet his life on half-assed logic.

He dropped the phone, hearing it clunk on the cement surface.

"Kick it over here."

When he did, the guy crushed it under his heel. He was a tough-looking character with buzz-cut hair, a knife scar slashing across his chin, and steely blue eyes. He looked like a mobster.

Mack had told Grant that Jenny must have had legitimate motives for running. This thug looked like an excellent reason.

Too bad he and Grant hadn't exchanged a little more information the last time they'd talked. He'd thought they'd have time later.

"Don't shoot," he said in a quavering voice as he hunched his shoulders, still trying to give the impression that he was an unfortunate bystander.

"Who are you calling?"

"The management. I need to get to my office, and they locked the building."

"What do you do?"

Christ, he had no idea what they did at this company, and the initials were no clue. For all he knew, they could be breeding earthworms and shipping them to biology classes, but he said, "IT."

"Okay, you're coming with me."

"Where?"

"Shut up if you don't want to get your head blown off."

Mack clamped his lips together. Turning, he walked ahead of the gunman back toward the Decorah patient facility.

"Open the door and walk down the hall."

He did, skirting the security desk and ending up in the room with the comatose patients. The other two gunmen were there, holding Terry Montrose, the orderly, and Lily at gunpoint.

A spurt of hope flashed across her face when she spotted Mack. Then she saw that his hands were raised, and the third gunman was in back of him.

When she started to speak, he gave a small shake of his head, and she closed her mouth.

The guy who had brought him in frisked him—and found the weapon in his shoulder holster.

"What have we here, Mr. IT guy?" he said in a sarcastic voice.

"I have it for protection."

"A lot of good it did you," the thug sneered.

Mack swung his gaze to the other two men. They were similar types, well-built men who looked like they could handle themselves in a fight. One of them was bald. The other had an Asian cast to his eyes and jet-black hair pulled back in a short queue.

"Over there," Buzz Cut said. It looked like he was the one in charge.

Mack gave the captors a fearful look and walked toward Lily and Terry.

"I don't know these people," he said. "This isn't fair. Why am I here?"

"Fair, yeah right," the head thug said with a sneer in his voice. "You were at the wrong place at the wrong time."

"We don't have any street drugs here," Lily said.

"We're not after drugs."

"Then what do you want?"

CHAPTER NINE

"Jenny Seaver," the guy said.

"Who?" Lily asked.

"Don't play dumb with me." Buzz Cut looked at the other two guys. "See which bed she's in."

Buzz Cut kept them covered while his companions began walking through the rows of beds, looking at the patients.

After long moments, the two henchmen returned to their boss. "She ain't in one of the beds I checked," the Asian guy said.

"Me neither," baldy echoed.

"You sure?"

"Yeah."

Buzz turned to the captives, "Who's in charge?"

"I am," Lily answered.

"Where is she?"

"Who?"

"I told you. Jenny Seaver."

"We've never had anyone here with that name."

"You're lying."

Terry spoke up in a voice he couldn't quite hold steady. "We had a Jenny Seville."

"Okay maybe she changed her name. Describe her."

"She's in her early or mid-twenties, I think. She had blue eyes, short caramel-colored hair."

"Yeah, that's her. Where is she?"

"She left—against medical advice," Lily answered.

Mack had been waiting for the right moment to contact his brother. The exchange about Jenny seemed like his best bet. While the conversation was going on, he turned slightly away, desperately sending his thoughts out to Grant.

What? Grant asked, sounding impatient when he heard the voice invade his mind.

We have a big problem. When I pulled into the parking lot at the Decorah Facility, I saw guys with assault rifles go in there. I pretended I was heading for the DSR unit, but one of them came after me and brought me back.

Christ.

Call Decorah. I can't keep talking now. They're going to think I'm doing something weird.

Get back to me when you can.

Grant looked up to see Jenny's eyes riveted to his face. "Something bad happened."

"The medical facility is under attack."

"By whom?"

"Men with assault rifles."

"Looking for me, I'm sure. I told you something like that could happen. I was right."

"I'm not going to waste time arguing with you now."

Pulling out his phone, he called the Decorah main number. The canned voice from the phone company said that the circuits were busy.

He tried again and got the same response.

Christ, was this a systematic attack where the bad guys had wiped out the agency?

"Now what?" Jenny asked when she saw the frustration on his face.

"I can't get hold of Decorah," he answered, trying to keep the panic out of his voice.

"Why not?"

"I guess we'll find out."

He was heading toward the door when he stopped short, caught in a dilemma.

Once again, Jenny reacted to his look. "What?"

He answered with a curse, then elaborated. "I don't want to drag you into danger, but I can't leave you here because I think you'll disappear again, and this time I'm afraid I won't find you."

She didn't contradict him.

"Running away now isn't the answer."

"Why not?" she asked in a defiant voice

"Because the bad thing you were afraid of has already happened."

She winced.

"Come on. We're wasting time."

"And what are we going to do when we get there?"

"I don't know."

Grim-faced, he marched her out of the room and toward the car. Silently he cursed the situation—and his lack of preparation. He always contacted the office through the main line. And if not, he could always get Mack on their private mental connection. That was why he didn't have cell phone numbers for any of the other guys.

"Shit."

He appreciated that she didn't interrupt while he tried to think himself out of the quicksand.

She'd asked what he was going to do when he got to the patient facility. He couldn't exactly drag Jenny in there, not where she was the one the bad guys were obviously looking for.

Back in the car, he held up his cell phone. "You're going to have to alert someone from Decorah."

"Who?"

"The first guy you can reach." He found the information number in the system and thought for a moment. Frank was only available through the office number. "Maybe the most efficient thing is to start with the Marshalls."

"Marshals?" she asked. "Like in the Old West?"

"No. A bunch of the guys who work for Decorah are cousins and have the same last name. Start with Cole Marshall. If you can't get him, try Brand Marshall. Or Rafe Marshall." He didn't explain that the Marshall cousins were all werewolves. That would be too much information at the wrong time.

As he drove toward Beltsville, he heard her talking to the information operator. Or maybe she was talking to a robot.

Just as they reached the turn into the industrial park, she said, "Okay, got it—301-555-2130."

"Who is it?"

"Brand."

He waited with his pulse pounding in his ears while the phone rang. Then he heard the werewolf answer, "Grant?"

"Just a minute." Jenny handed him the phone.

"Problem?" his friend asked.

"Yeah. I can't get through to the main Decorah number, and there's a situation."

Quickly he explained that the patient facility was under attack—from three gunmen, most likely looking for Jenny.

"I'll get a counterforce together as quickly as possible," the other agent promised, then paused. "Don't go in 'til we get there."

"I ..."

"There's no point in your getting captured, too—or killed."

He wanted to pound the wheel in frustration because he knew that Brand was right. With his lips set in a grim line, he pulled over to the side of the access road, several yards from the Decorah building.

He felt Jenny's eyes on him.

"Like I kept saying in the first place, this is my fault," she whispered.

"No. It's the fault of the guy who kidnapped you. Your only sin was getting away from them."

She didn't answer, and they sat in tense silence waiting for reinforcements to appear.

Jesus, no!

The mental shout of agony came from Mack.

CHAPTER TEN

Stay cool, Grant silently ordered.

"What happened?" Jenny gasped as she read the sick look on his face.

"One of the guys just hit Lily. I'm afraid Mack is gonna do something stupid—like get himself killed."

Do what it takes to stay alive, he mentally shouted. He wanted to stay in contact, but he knew he couldn't affect the scene in the lab from here. Instead he focused on the woman beside him, torn in two directions. He couldn't lose Mack. And he couldn't lose Jenny. But could he trust her?

"I have to go in there. Give me your word that you won't run."

He saw her internal struggle reflected on her face. Finally she gave him the right answer. "Okay. I won't run," she said in a flat voice.

"Get in the backseat. Down on the floor where no one can see you."

"And be a coward?"

His voice turned fierce. "That's not being a coward. I have to focus, and I can't do it if I'm worried about you."

"Okay,"

Hoping she wasn't lying, he pocketed his keys, jumped out of the car and started for the building.

* * *

Jenny climbed out of the passenger seat and into the back of the car. Her heart was in her throat as she watched Grant move toward the medical facility. He looked like a man who was caught between speed, urgency and the knowledge that he could end up dead in the next few moments.

He turned back, and when he saw her still sitting up, he gave her a fierce look. She nodded and scooted to the floor, hating that she was using none of the skills she'd acquired while she'd been in the VR. A lot of good they were doing her when all she could manage now was to hide. But she did understand Grant's point of view. And she'd given him enough grief for one evening.

She had been in turmoil ever since he'd knocked on her motel room door, and she'd met him with a gun in her hand. The look in his eyes had made her heart squeeze painfully. He'd been angry, hurt, worried about her. There was no way she could have shot him, but when she'd put the gun down, she'd braced for him to slap her, or shake her, or show his anger in some physical way as her kidnapper would have done.

She'd gotten used to living with violence, and she'd been half afraid all men were like that. Now she knew for sure that Grant Bradley was different. Instead of lashing out, he'd wrapped her close and let her cry in his arms.

Now he was hurtling headlong toward danger—danger that she had provoked. She simply couldn't get away from that fact.

Unable to cower on the floor, she popped up again, her gaze zeroing in on him as he reached the entrance to the building, flattened himself against the wall and cautiously looked around the corner, then darted back out of the line of sight.

It took all her willpower to stay in the car. She wanted to *do something*. Yet at the same time, she knew he was right. If she got caught, all of this would have been for nothing.

She kept her gaze glued to Grant. He was moving forward again, and she tensed, sure he was about to go into the building. At that moment, a headlight in the rearview mirror made her head swing around. Two cars were coming down the narrow road. The drivers switched off their lights when they were still behind her.

Who were they? The men Brand Marshall had brought? Or reinforcements for the bad guys?

She saw Grant whirl as the lead car approached. Then she could tell from his posture that it was the Decorah men who had arrived.

The vehicle glided to a stop. Several men got out and conferred with Grant.

One of them rounded the car, and she couldn't see what he was doing on the other side. Moments later, a big dog—it must have been a dog—trotted into the street. Men stopped beside him, putting something onto the front of his head. It looked like a camera. Maybe the dog was going to be their eyes and ears inside the patient facility.

Grant reached to open the door, and the animal slipped in.

She should go back to her position on the floor, but she simply couldn't do it.

The situation was rapidly slipping out of control. Lily raised her hand to her cheek, pressing against the stinging slap the leader of the thugs had delivered. She looked from the man who had slapped her to the patients and back again. She'd agreed to be the director here to give these people a safe place after she'd realized Dr. Hamilton was using them for his own purposes. In the time it took to grab a quick breath, everything had changed—for her and them.

When Mack shouted, "Leave her the hell alone," her attention snapped to him.

Buzz Cut tipped his head to the side, staring at him. "You said you didn't know these people. It sounds like you care about this broad."

When Mack didn't answer, the man smiled. "What's she to you—your sweetie?"

Lily willed Mack not to answer and make things worse. But they were going rapidly downhill on their own.

"I don't like to see women abused," he answered through gritted teeth.

"We can change things around if that's gonna work better," the thug said. Turning to one of his men, he ordered, "Grab him."

Lily wanted to scream, but she knew it was only going to make her look weak.

While the other henchman kept his gun trained on the group of captives, the Asian guy came around behind Mack and grabbed his hands. The leader also put down his weapon on the desk. Taking a step forward, he drew back his hand, then punched Mack in the gut.

He doubled over, gasping for breath.

"Stop it!" Lily cried out.

Ignoring the plea, the thug went on in a conversational tone, "Sounds like we have a nice situation going here. He cares about you. And you care about him."

"You animal," she whispered under her breath.

"What's that?"

"Nothing." She turned her head, trying to judge Mack's condition.

His face took on a look that could have meant his thoughts had turned inward. But she knew him too well for that. He was reaching out to his brother.

Was Grant already here? And if so, what could he do against three armed men who were holding hostages?

She tried to read Mack's expression, but he was keeping it deliberately neutral.

"You want me to start shooting patients?" the ringleader asked like he was a teacher considering adding to a homework assignment because the members of the class had been giving him a hard time. "Which one should I take out first? How about that slack-jawed girl in the corner with the drool on her chin? She looks pretty worthless."

Lily couldn't hold back a gasp. He was talking about her sister, Shelly. "No. Please."

"Then tell me where you're hiding Jenny Seaver."

Lily fought her fear and frustration. "I'm not hiding her. I was telling you the truth. She disappeared while I was busy."

Buzz Cut thought about it while the one who had been holding Mack turned him loose and came back to join his friends.

Mack wavered on his feet but stayed standing.

The leader looked at the three captives. "Okay, I've got another idea that might make you talk," he said, addressing Mack. Turning to Lily, he ordered, "Take off your clothes."

She couldn't believe that she'd heard him right. "What?"

"Take off your clothes. The guys and I want to see what you've got. And if you can't give us Jenny, you might as well give us some fun."

To her horror, Lily saw the anger flare on Mack's face. My God, if he did something stupid like speaking up again he could get himself killed. "Don't," she murmured.

He was turned toward her, and his lips formed one word. "Stall."

She acknowledged with a small nod.

Probably Buzz Cut was enjoying lording it over this group of helpless people. Maybe he was even glad that he had to exert some pressure to find Jenny. Obviously he thought he was totally in charge. She prayed he was going to be very surprised when he found out how wrong he was.

Trying to draw out the moment, Lily took a step back, thrust out her chest, and raised her head like a performer on stage. She could tell from the way the bad guys were watching that they liked the little show, yet this wasn't a part she really knew how to play.

"Hurry up," Buzz Cut ordered.

Unable to look at the thug, she kept her gaze focused somewhere over his shoulder as her hands went to the front of her scrub shirt.

She didn't have to pretend her fingers were shaking as she fumbled with the buttons

All of the men with guns were focused on her, and she saw something they didn't. At the far end of the reception area, the door had eased open. Moments later, a wolf stuck its head around the security desk in the anteroom. The animal had to be one of the Marshalls. They had sent him in to scope out the interior.

There was something attached to the top of his head. As he swung from side to side, she realized it must be a camera. He came quietly down the hall, paused in the doorway for several moments, and then silently backed up.

CHAPTER ELEVEN

Lily had felt a spurt of hope when she saw the wolf. She couldn't stop her spirits from sinking as she watched him withdraw.

Her attention zinged back to her chief captor when he snapped, "Get on with it, or I'm gonna help you out."

Knowing his patience was wearing thin, she closed her eyes for a moment, steeling herself to keep the performance going as long as she had to. But what if that meant taking off all her clothes and letting the goons drag her into the next room?

Struggling to thrust that thought out of her mind, she finished unbuttoning the top, then began to tug it off her shoulders so that her only garment above the waist was her bra. Thank God she'd worn a practical one this morning. Not one of the lacy numbers that Mack liked.

The men watched with greedy expressions, undoubtedly anticipating what they were going to do to her.

"Take that off too. Let's see your tits," one of them shouted.

It was then that she saw the door ease open again and armed Decorah Security men coming into the front of the facility, taking up positions. But she knew they couldn't shoot, not when the three hostages were in the line of fire.

Lily struggled to keep up her performance and hold the thugs attention as she sensuously reached behind her, fingering the hooks at the back of her bra.

It was all working—until one of the invaders must have sensed movement behind him. Or perhaps her expression had changed enough to alert him to danger. He whirled and lay down a blast of automatic gunfire.

The others turned as well, blasting away.

As the shooting started, Mack's gaze swept the room in frustration. Lily knew he was searching for a weapon. Before he could get himself killed, she grabbed his arm and pulled him toward the dressing room. He gave her a surprised look, then let her tug him out of the line of fire. When they were in the dressing area, he turned the tables, yanking her to the floor. As bullets slammed into the doorframe, he came down on top of her, shielding her body from the barrage.

Terry leaped in seconds behind them, hitting the floor farther back in the room and hugging the cold tiles with his arms over his head.

Beyond the dressing room, Grant and the other Decorah agents exchanged fire with the bad guys.

Brand ducked low behind the security desk, using it as a shield as he kept firing. He saw one of the bad guys go down. The other two kept shooting, both of them moving toward the lobby, laying down fire as they went. The Decorah men were forced back. One of the invaders was stuck in the reception area. The other barreled toward the door, spraying a steady stream of fire that kept the rescuers pinned down.

They were unable to drop him, and he exited the building.

Brand, who was closest to the main room, charged into the patient area, intent on making sure the captives were okay.

The other two Decorah men leaped toward the exit and kept firing at the fleeing man, but he forced them to take cover as he returned fire.

Inside the dressing room, Mack continued to shield Lily with his body. She pressed her hands over her ears, trying to dampen the sound of the gun battle and praying that the bad guys weren't coming in to shoot Mack.

The barrage seemed to go on for a century. Then the sound of the automatic weapons receded into the distance. When the clatter of the assault rifles stopped, she could hear running feet. Mack started to get up.

"No," she shouted as he scrambled to his feet.

He yanked himself free and grabbed the bench, holding it in front of himself as he moved toward the door.

Before he reached it, Brand Marshall charged in.

"All clear." His gaze swept over them. "You all right?"

"Yes," they answered.

Mack put down the bench and helped Lily to her feet. From the shelves she grabbed another scrub suit top and put it on so that she was covered up again.

After the clatter of the assault rifles, the facility was strangely quiet.

When she stepped into the main room, two of the invaders were lying in pools of blood on the tile floor, one near where he had originally been standing, and the other closer to the door.

She didn't see the third man, the one she'd called Buzz Cut.

"What happened?" Mack asked, looking at the Decorah men. It seemed that on short notice, Grant had been able to round up Brand and Cole Marshall, plus Wyatt Granger.

Brand answered. "We got one of them right away. The other two took cover, then started pushing their way into the lobby area, shooting as they came. We got two of them. The other escaped.

She looked at the two dead men. "The leader was the one who got away."

"Okay."

Lily went into the supply room, found two sheets and draped them over the dead men.

"The head guy was one fierce bastard," Brand said. "It looked like he was determined to escape—or get killed."

She looked at the Decorah agents, then turned toward Mack "Where's Grant?"

"He went to make sure Jenny's safe."

Lily stared around the ruined facility. "Thank God the patients were at the side of the room. But we'd better check to make sure none of them and none of the life support equipment was hit," she said to Terry.

As she spoke, she hurried to her sister's bed. Shelly was lying there as peacefully as if nothing had happened. It was always so strange to see what she really looked like. In the VR, she was a little girl—the same age as when she'd gone into a coma. But in the real world, her body had matured into an adult's. And when Lily saw her like this, she couldn't help thinking about how different her sister's life could have been.

Lily laid a hand on Shelly's brow, then touched the pulse in her neck, reassured by the steady rhythm. As she checked the telemetry, she spoke softly to her sister, even though she knew Shelly wasn't going to respond. "Thank God you're okay."

When she'd made sure Shelly was fine, she turned back to see how Terry was doing. He hardly looked in condition to check anything, but he dutifully began going from bed to bed, following her orders, making sure that everybody was okay and all the equipment was operational.

When he caught his breath, she gave him a questioning look. "What?"

"Jonas Corker took a bullet."

"How is he?"

"Dead."

"Oh no."

She'd left him in a bed close to the center of the room, and he'd been in the line of fire.

"I'm sorry," Mack said. "But I think he wasn't going to work out, anyway."

"Yes, but ..."

"We have to worry about the living now," her husband clipped out.

"Right." Lily focused on the Decorah men. "All of you are okay?"

"I could use a bandage on my arm, so I don't keep dripping blood on this shirt," Wyatt Granger said.

Lily crossed to him and saw blood oozing through the fabric of his sleeve.

"Take off your shirt."

"It's just a graze."

"We'll see."

Wyatt unbuttoned and shrugged out of his shirt, and she looked at the wound. "Okay, you're right."

"Yeah, I can move it."

"But you still need a bandage and antibiotics."

She had just finished with Wyatt when movement in the doorway made her head snap up.

Jenny was standing there, not quite steady on her feet, clutching Grant's hand. She was dressed in Lily's clothes and looking like she wished she was on the other side of the continental United States.

Her gaze skidded to the white sheets on the floor, then quickly away again.

When she caught Lily's eye, she looked like she was going to cry. Straightening her shoulders, she said, "I'm sorry."

Everything had been happening so fast that Lily hadn't know what she would do or say when they brought Jenny back—if they could bring her back. But here she was, looking like she'd survived an earthquake.

Lily opened her mouth and heard herself remarking, "Running away wasn't the smartest thing you ever did."

The young woman lowered her head. "I can see that now. I didn't know what else to do."

"You could have trusted us," Grant said in a gritty voice.

She kept her focus downward as she spoke. "The whole time I was in the VR, I thought I was putting you all in danger. And I was right," she added, sweeping her arm around the carnage.

"We would have been better prepared if you'd leveled with us," Grant said, not making it any easier on her.

She dragged in a breath and let it out before saying, "I understand that now."

"How long were you planning your—escape?" Lily asked.

"I don't know." She kept her gaze on Lily. "You knew I was waking up."

"Yes."

"I was trying to play it down so you wouldn't realize I was so close to the surface. And I started thinking I could get away. Like Mack did."

"I didn't advise that for him, either," Lily continued. "Let me check you out."

"Don't' make me go back into the VR," Jenny said.

"We'll see."

To get away from their audience, she gathered up a stethoscope and other equipment and ushered Jenny down the hall to the staff lounge.

"Sit down," she said, sweeping her arm toward the bed where she sometimes slept if she had to stay on duty.

Jenny remained on her feet. "I stole your purse and your clothes—and your car," she murmured.

"I won't say 'that's okay.' But I think I understand. You thought you were getting us out of danger—even when you were putting your own welfare at risk. But those guys came here, and they thought we were lying about your leaving. When they didn't find you, they started threatening us. They were going to kill patients to get us to talk."

Jenny winced. "I guess I wasn't thinking straight. I figured that if they came here and didn't find me, they'd go away."

"Who were they?"

A voice chimed in from the doorway. "Yeah, maybe you'd better give us some details."

Jenny and Lily both looked up to see Grant standing in the doorway, a hard expression on his face.

Jenny gave Lily a panicked look.

"Let's not press her now," she said to Grant. "She's been through an ordeal. She needs to sleep."

Jenny opened her mouth and closed it again, looking relieved.

Grant withdrew, and Lily listened to Jenny's heart and lungs, checked her reflexes, palpated her stomach and went through all the other simple tests of the girl's physical state.

"How am I?" Jenny asked.

"In remarkably good shape. It looks like all the physical training you were doing in there carried over into the real world."

"I was hoping it would."

"How did you feel when you got up?"

"Shaky," Jenny admitted.

"Not dizzy?"

"No." She cleared her throat. "But I decided I couldn't drive very far. That's how Grant found me."

"He was really worried," Lily said sternly.

"I know." She raised her head to Lily. "So do I have to go back into the VR?"

"At this point, I'm not sure what good it would do. But you do need to rest. "I'm going to give you a sedative," Lily said. "If you're not going back to the Mirador, at least you need to sleep."

"Okay."

Jenny sat on one of the beds, and Lily gave her a couple of strong sedative pills. After swallowing them, she slipped under the covers and lay down.

Lily stayed until the girl was sleeping. Then she turned off the light and closed the door. She had a lot of questions for Jenny, but probably not as many as Grant.

CHAPTER TWELVE

Carlos Mardano was ten miles away before he turned off the highway and into a development of low-end houses. He found a dead-end street and pulled to a stop in front of a rancher where all the lights were off. Of course in this kind of neighborhood, someone could come out with a shotgun and ask what he was doing there, but in that case, he'd give them a big surprise.

He breathed out a sigh and wiped the sweat from his forehead, then threw back his head, thinking about what had just happened. Danny and Lee were both dead, but he'd been able to get away—partly through their stupidity. They'd made themselves targets while he had hung back, then taken the opportunity to dash through the door.

The question was—would he have been better off joining them? Because they were already dead, they didn't have to face Rambo's wrath.

What were his options?

He could keep driving, head for some big city and look for work among the gangs and mob organizations. But there was no guarantee that someone greedy for money wouldn't turn him in to Rambo. And then he'd wish he'd been shot in the firefight and gotten it over quickly.

He could try to pass for a civilian and disappear into some small town in the Midwest where he could get a legit job. His dad had been a plumber. He'd helped out on some jobs. Maybe he could work his way into that trade. Or maybe he could be a farmer. He snorted. Both of those professions meant wading through shit—not his kind of scene.

Which left him with the alternative—go back to Rambo and say that he'd failed. Or—not failed.

How could he spin this disaster to his advantage? And how could he turn the tables on the bitch who'd been leading him on by starting to undress when she knew her friends were coming to the rescue.

All along, he'd thought she was giving him a song and dance. At least he'd seen from the expression on her face that she was lying about something. And what good would it do her to lie about anything besides Jenny Seaver? Probably she knew where the little idiot was. Which meant he could find her. All he had to do was tell Rambo they'd hidden Jenny; and if they kept watch on the facility, they'd find her. Of course, he couldn't do that by himself. He'd need more guys—to make sure he had the place covered twenty-four seven.

Yeah, that was the best way to go.

It sounded like a reasonable plan. The sticking point was going back to Rambo and twisting defeat into anticipated victory.

Yet even as he bolstered his case, he couldn't dismiss a nagging worry. You could do the perfectly logical thing with Rambo, and the guy would react in some out-of-kilter way.

Again Carlos thought about taking off. Christ, he wasn't really sure which way to jump. Closing his eyes, he cursed the day he'd gone to work for the guy. He'd been tempted by the pay, but he hadn't realized the working conditions would be almost intolerable.

Grant came back to the patient area and saw the other Decorah men putting the bad guys into body bags. He'd been in firefights before, but never inside a building where he worked.

"Are we going to call the cops?" he asked.

"I think not." The answer came from Frank Decorah who strode into the main room and looked around at the mess.

"You figure nobody noticed the gun battle?" Grant asked. "Or they thought we were filming a made-for-TV movie?"

Frank shook his head. "I think we're lucky as hell that we're the only tenant in this industrial park that operates on a twenty-four hour basis."

"I suppose you picked the location for that reason," Mack said.

"Yeah. I wanted as much privacy as possible, given that we'd already battled a gang of thugs and the FBI at Hamilton's old lab."

Grant kept his gaze on the boss. "When I knew the place was under attack, I tried to call the main Decorah number. Did the bad guys take it out—or what?"

"No. It was a phone company problem."

Grant kept his gaze on his boss. "Which could have gotten Lily, Mack and Terry killed. Is there some way we can have a direct line to you—if we need it?"

Frank looked torn. "I've never operated that way. But under the circumstances, I think it's necessary. I'll get a dedicated cell phone and make sure everybody has the number."

There were murmurs of agreement and thanks around the room.

Frank glanced toward the hallway "I want some answers from Jenny Seville."

"Her real name is Jenny Seaver," Terry said. "We found that out from the men who came looking for her."

Frank nodded, "That's a start. Maybe it will lead to a lot more information."

He turned to Lily. "How long before she wakes up?"

"At least six hours."

"Okay. We can use the time to do some planning and get this place back into shape."

"Including patching up the bullet holes?" Mark asked.

"Yeah. Otherwise we're going to have to explain how they got there."

"And explain how one of the patients got killed?" Lily asked.

His gaze jerked to her. "We lost a patient?"

"Yes, the man we tried to introduce to the VR. His bed was closest to the gun battle."

"He's the man who went nuts?" Frank clarified.

"Yes."

"I hate to be pragmatic, but he might be better off now."

Lily winced, but she silently acknowledged that Frank was probably right.

But he must have read her expression. "We'll find another suitable candidate, and you can try again. And next time, he won't be caught in the middle of a gun battle."

"Yes."

Frank kept his gaze on Lily. "We've got to have a death certificate."

She nodded.

"I know you hated finding out that Dr. Hamilton was running an illegal operation. But in this case, it's probably better to say he died of heart failure."

She thought about it for a few moments. Frank was right. She didn't like doing something illegal. But she knew it was better to leave gun violence out of the equation.

"Okay," she answered in a low voice.

Grant shifted his weight from one foot to the other, and the rest if the group turned toward him. "I think we'd better clear out of here," he said. "I mean, one of the guys escaped. He could come back with reinforcements."

Alarm flashed in Lily's eyes. "You don't mean tonight?"

"Probably not. It depends on where he's from. And what kind of instructions he gets from his boss."

"We need to find out who that is," Mack muttered.

"I'll put Teddy on it while we deal with the current situation," Frank answered, referring to one of the Decorah IT men.

"And where do you suggest we move the patients?" Lily asked.

"There's room in the main Decorah facility," Frank answered. "It will be crowded, but it's only temporary. And just to be on the safe side, we'll have at least five Decorah agents in the building at all times."

There was agreement around the room.

"Meanwhile, we'll get this place back in shape." Frank looked at the bullet-riddled security desk. "We might as well throw that thing out."

"My cousin Ross has some experience in the construction trade," Brand said.

"Okay, call him." Frank looked at Mack, "And call a private ambulance service to transport the patients."

"We have to set up the beds first," Lily said. "And do it in shifts."

"How many extra do you have?"

"Four."

So far, they had been making plans for the patient facility. Now Grant looked at the two dead men. "What about the bodies?"

Frank followed his gaze. "We've left bodies scattered around before."

"Yeah, like in upstate New York," Brand agreed.

"But never in our own front yard."

"Somebody's gonna miss them," Grant said.

"Nobody who wants to get the authorities involved."

Grant grimaced. "But we can't just leave them here."

"I brought a van," Frank said. He turned to Lily. "We need DNA samples so we can try to identify them."

She went to a supply cabinet, got out the equipment she needed, and turned to one of the body bags.

Mack and Grant exchanged glances as she got to work.

She's come a long way since she first worked for Hamilton, Grant observed.

Yeah, his brother allowed.

Grant nodded, then closed off his mind from his brother. But he knew Mack had caught his fleeting thought that he wished Jenny were as straightforward as his brother's wife. Of course, Lily had been following Hamilton's directions when she'd first met Mack—before she'd started working with Mack.

When Lily had finished getting the samples, the agents loaded the thugs in the van.

"And now what?" Mack asked when they'd closed the doors of the vehicle.

"Then you let me worry about it," his boss answered.

Grant looked toward the comatose patients "You can't just put dead guys into a virtual reality and make them disappear," he said.

A strange expression crossed Frank Decorah's face, but all he said was, "I'll be back as soon as I can. While I'm gone, move the spare beds to the Decorah headquarters and put Teddy on the Jenny Seaver problem."

Grant nodded. He was having his own thoughts about what to do next, but he wasn't going to start working on anything until Frank returned.

CHAPTER THIRTEEN

Grant had been up for more than twenty-four hours and finally conked out in a leather recliner in the staff lounge at the main Decorah office.

He'd tried to stay awake, reviewing the plans the team had made, but when he'd closed his eyes for a moment, he was gone.

Mack gave his brother a long look, then went off to scroll through commercial news feeds on one of the office desktop computers. As far as anyone could see, there was no mention on the local or national news of the shoot-out—or of any men missing.

Grant woke up when Frank came back from his private mission after about three hours. None of the Decorah staff asked him what he'd done with the bodies. But Grant assumed they were somewhere nobody was going to stumble over them. His home was next to the Beltsville Agricultural acreage. Grant pictured the Decorah head taking the limp forms to an unused part of the compound and burying them under some long-forgotten hybrid azalea experiment. Only that was just a fantasy. He was sure Frank was too smart to dispose of anybody on federal land, where discovery could lead back to him and Decorah Security.

Grant breathed out a small sigh. A visit from the police was probably off the table, but there were plenty more things to worry about.

Since the attack on the patient facility, Grant had done a lot of things he wasn't proud of. But he'd told himself they were necessary to save Jenny—maybe save her from herself. When Lily had given her a sedative, she'd said that she was only going to sleep for six hours. But after Frank returned, Grant put his case to the group, and they basically agreed with his analysis of the situation.

The first order of business had been to inject Jenny with a sedative that would keep her sleeping for an additional six hours, to give them time to get ready to interrogate her. Then they moved her from the scene of the shoot-out to the main Decorah building where they could keep her under guard along with the patients who had also been moved.

As the time drew near to wake her, Grant used the washroom, then splashed cold water on his face, thinking he still looked pretty rough. Stepping into the hall, he was mentally preparing for the hours to come when a scream from the room where Jenny was sleeping had everybody snap to alert status.

"Christ." Grant grabbed the Sig in his shoulder holster.

With the others trailing behind, he went running down the hall to the room where they'd stashed her. Gun in hand, he plowed through the door. The room was in semidarkness. But to his relief, he saw at once that Jenny was alone. He could see she was thrashing her head back and forth on the pillow, obviously caught in the clutches of a bad dream.

He turned to Mack, who was right behind him.

"Nightmare."

"Yeah."

His twin went back to the conference room. Putting the gun on the floor outside the room, Grant stepped inside and closed the door behind himself.

In her sleep, Jenny had kicked her covers off, her head was moving restlessly, and her face was contorted into a mask of fear.

Crossing the room, he sat down on the side of the bed.

"Jenny," he called out softly as he reached to clasp his hand around her shoulder.

She didn't seem to hear him, and he tightened his grip.

The pressure must have gotten her attention. Her eyes snapped open, but she didn't focus on him. Instead, she seemed to be looking at some mental scene that he couldn't see.

"Jenny," he tried again,

She shook off his hand and lunged toward him, her hands going for his neck. It was a quick, deadly attack, and his only choice was to grab her arms as he pushed her back onto the bed. But she'd been learning defensive techniques from him, and she bucked him away, springing up and coming after him again.

"Jenny, it's Grant," he called. But she didn't seem to hear him as she kicked out, knocking his legs out from under him.

He went down on the floor. As he came back up, he was scrambling to keep her from reaching for his neck again. But she changed tactics, and he could see she was rearing back for a head butt.

When he danced back out of range, she struggled to keep her balance.

Once again, he tried her name.

"Jenny, don't. It's Grant."

She'd been fighting with a desperate determination. Now she seemed to hear him. For the first time, her gaze focused on his face. He could tell the moment she recognized who he was. Her eyes went wide, and her mouth opened in a startled gasp.

Pushing herself away, she ended up tumbling onto the bed where she scrambled up and pressed her back to the wall.

"Oh my God, Grant, I hurt you."

"I'm all right."

He moved cautiously to her side. When she didn't flinch, he gathered her to him, rocking her in his arms as his hands soothed over her back and shoulders.

"You were having a nightmare," he murmured.

"Yes."

"What was it about?"

"He had sent his men after me. I was trying to get away, but there was nowhere to hide. I'd go into a room, and it would have no windows."

"Who?" he asked. "Who sent men after you?"

She hesitated for a moment. "Rambo."

"The guy in the movie?"

"No. That's what they call him."

"Okay."

She tipped her face downward, and he was sure she thought she had given away some secret that should stay hidden.

"It's fine," he said.

She shook her head, looking miserable—and so vulnerable that he wanted to lift her chin up so that he could kiss her. But he wasn't going to do it. When he had made love with her in the VR, he'd convinced himself that she felt the same way about him as he did about her. Too bad their last few encounters had left him feeling like he hardly knew her.

He held her for a few more moments, then eased away. "Everybody is waiting to talk to you."

"I'm going to be the center of attention?"

"We need your input."

She looked even more miserable, and he wished he could have just told her the staff was having a meal in the lounge. But that would have been a lie. They were waiting to find out what she knew about the attack.

104

He stood up. "Why don't you get dressed and come out. We'll talk."

"Okay," she answered in a small voice, and it was hard to believe she was the same woman as the fierce warrior who had attacked him when he'd woken her from the dream.

"I got you some clothes," he said.

"You did?"

"Yeah. It was fun picking some stuff I thought you'd like. I'll let you get dressed. If you want to take a shower, you can do that first. We'll be in the lounge." He cleared his throat. "I mean the lounge at the main Decorah building. The other place was too messed up to use. We moved everyone over here while we get the patient facility in shape again."

"You moved me while I was sleeping?"

"Yes. Like I said, the patient facility is a wreck. And it's safer here."

He started to say that they were keeping five armed men on hand at all times in case the guy who had gotten away came back. But he stopped himself just in time.

"I'll take a shower," she said. Probably she felt grungy after her escape from the VR. But probably she also wanted to postpone the meeting with the Decorah staff.

"We're down the hall. Turn right and keep walking. You can't miss it."

"I'll hurry," she said, then scooted into the bathroom and locked the door. To give her some privacy, he went back to the others.

"Well?" Mack asked.

"Nightmare."

"Figures."

"How long will she be?"

"She doesn't want to come out here. But on the other hand, she probably wants to get the questions over with. I did get something out of her. The guy who sent the goons is called Rambo."

"That's good because Seaver was a real dead end."

"We can hardly look up Rambo," Teddy Granada from the IT department put in.

"Try it by state. Maybe it's a nickname for an underworld character."

"And maybe it will turn out to be someone more accessible."

After she heard a door close, Jenny poked her head out of the bathroom. When she saw that Grant was gone, she crossed the room and turned the lock.

She felt strange doing it, and yet she didn't feel safe either. The nightmare proved it. And to be truthful, she wasn't feeling so great about Grant. He said that everyone was waiting to talk to her. She could imagine they had been thinking of questions to ask while she was sleeping.

She wished she had a watch. Lily had said she was going to sleep for six hours, but somehow it felt longer than that.

And then there was Grant's admission that they'd moved her to a different place while she was sedated. The Decorah headquarters building, he'd said. She'd never been there, but she assumed it wasn't that far away from the place where they kept the stiffs.

She laughed. The stiffs. Nice way to put it. Until a few hours ago, she'd been one of them.

Before returning to the bathroom, she went to the closet. She found underwear on shelves, along with a selection of shirts and slacks. She took a bra and panties, jeans and a dark-blue knit top into the bathroom. After using the facilities she brushed her teeth, took a shower and dried her hair—all the while trying to plan out what she was going to say.

She peered at herself in the mirror. When she'd first come out of the VR, she'd felt and looked a lot worse than when she'd been inside. Now she was feeling more like herself—and looking better, too.

106

Would that make her feel more confident when facing a whole bunch of people who wanted answers to questions she wasn't prepared to give them?

CHAPTER FOURTEEN

Jenny had never liked being the center of attention. It had usually meant trouble, not praise. When she walked down the hall to the lounge, and six pairs of eyes looked up at her, she struggled not to cringe.

Her gaze swung around the group of men—and one woman, Lily Wardman. They were sitting on comfortable couches and in easy chairs that all were angled to face a flat-screen TV mounted on the wall at one side of the room. In addition to Lily, she also recognized Grant and Mack.

An older man stood up. He had salt and pepper hair and a lined face, but he was slim and fit. It must be Frank Decorah, and he looked like he was the equal of his agents. Grant had told her he'd been injured in Vietnam, but he didn't look old enough to have fought in that war.

"I'm Frank Decorah," he said, confirming her guess about his identity.

She nodded at him, then said quickly, "I'm sorry I caused so much trouble."

"Not your fault," he said. "You were unconscious when you got to the Hamilton Lab. Actually, Dr. Hamilton didn't ask for permission to get you into his program. So everything that's happened since has been out of your control."

She licked her lips. "Except running away."

"There is that."

A plump, messy-looking guy put down a plate with a couple of sandwiches. "I'm Teddy Granada. I'm on the IT staff."

She nodded in acknowledgment.

"And I'm Brand Marshall," another man said. "I'm one of the Decorah agents."

"You were one of the guys at the patient facility last night?"

"Yes."

"Nice to meet you," she said, although it was far from the truth.

"There are sandwiches and salads on the buffet," Frank Decorah said. "You're probably hungry."

Probably she should be, but her stomach was in knots. She went to the buffet and turned her back on the group while she got herself a tuna sandwich and a bottle of unsweetened iced tea.

When she came back, she took a seat in one of the easy chairs and put her sandwich and drink on the table to her right, wondering if she'd chosen the spot to isolate herself. She shot a quick glance toward Grant, but he was talking to Teddy Granada.

Nobody spoke while she took a few bites of her sandwich and sipped some of the iced tea.

Then Frank Decorah said, "There are surveillance cameras in the patient facility. We'd like you to take a look and tell us if you recognize the men who mounted the attack."

"What happened to them?"

"They're dead," Frank said in a flat voice.

"Okay."

"Some of the footage is disturbing," the Decorah director added.

"Actually, most of it," Lily warned.

"I understand," she said, wondering how bad it was going to be. Well, watching was part of her punishment for pulling the running-away stunt.

She pushed her sandwich to the side when the television picture flickered.

"This is what happened during the attack," Frank said.

She kept her gaze on the screen, seeing men with automatic rifles come into the lobby where she had exited when she stole Lily's car and drove away. She supposed if they'd wanted to make sure that nobody could identify them, they would have been wearing masks. But none of them had bothered to hide their faces. Probably that meant that they weren't planning to leave any witnesses.

She made a small sound when she saw the trio.

"You recognize them?" Frank asked.

"Yes."

"Who are they?"

"They work for a mobster in New Jersey," she answered.

"Who?"

She glanced toward Grant, then away. "I think they call him Rambo."

"Okay," Frank said. "And why do they want you?"

She closed her eyes and dragged in a breath before answering. "I was a teacher—working at a school in New Jersey."

"What school?" Frank asked.

"I don't want to get them in trouble."

"We need the information."

"Why?"

"Because we want to understand your background."

That was the crux of the problem. From the first moment she'd woken up with Lily, Grant, and a bunch of other strangers in the VR, she hadn't wanted to talk about her background. But now she had to cooperate or they were going to think something was weird.

"It's a private school called Fairview."

She could see the guy named Teddy typing the information into a tablet.

"What did you teach?" Frank asked.

"Fourth grade."

Frank nodded, and the guy who was taking notes wrote that down, too.

"Go on," Frank said.

"At a parent-teacher night, I met the father of one of my students."

"Who?"

She didn't want to tell this story, but it looked like she had no choice. Or—what if she refused? What would they do to her? Probably nothing threatening, but she wouldn't be able to stand the looks on their faces. Because she'd already put them through a lot, she took a sip of the tea and kept speaking. "He said his name was Gabe Thompson."

"You think he was lying about his name?"

"There's no way I can be sure."

"Okay. What happened?"

"He seemed to like me—and I liked him."

"Who was his child?"

"A boy named Liam. Gabe was divorced from his son's mother. They shared custody. The boy lived with his mom during the school year, but Gabe said he wanted to stay in his son's life. He met me after school several times, and then he asked me out. He seemed nice, so I agreed." She went on quickly, wanting to get it over with. "He told me a story about how they hadn't gotten along and agreed to split. I guess I wanted to believe it. We got more and more involved. I thought he was nice. I convinced myself that we were compatible. And when he asked me, I agreed to marry him."

"Did you love him?"

The question had come from Grant. Turning to him, she saw the intensity on his face. Quietly, she asked, "How is that relevant?"

"I'm trying to get the whole picture."

"I convinced myself I did," she said in a low voice. "Or enough to make a life with him. That turned out to be a mistake. I found out that the reason he got divorced was that his wife objected to Liam's being the son of a mob boss. Well, apparently he'd said he'd left that life behind him and was focusing on a legitimate business. But then he must have slid back into the lifestyle. When he was at his house, he'd get phone calls and excuse himself to talk. Or tough-looking men would show up."

She stopped, then started again. "When I told him I thought the relationship wasn't going to work out, he wouldn't allow me to leave. He kept me captive at his house."

"How could he do that?" Lily asked.

"I guess he could do anything he wanted."

"But you had a job. Didn't they expect you back at school?"

"I think he told them I was sick. I don't know all the details. All I knew was that he was ruthless, and he'd do whatever it took to get his way. And I knew that if I stayed with him, I'd eventually die inside. So I started looking for an opportunity to disappear. One afternoon, when he was out, I stole the keys to one of the cars on the property and I took off. I was driving recklessly, and you know what happened."

Lily nodded.

"Let's continue with the rest of the video," Grant said.

She gave him a quick glance, then looked away. With every fiber of her being, she wished she could tell him she didn't want to see it, but she already felt like a total jerk for staying in the car while he crept up on the patient facility to wait for the other Decorah agents.

It was almost impossible for her to keep her eyes on the screen, but she forced herself to watch one of the thugs slap Lily and punch Grant in the stomach. Then Lily was forced to start taking off her clothes. Jenny felt her whole body go cold as she took in the performance, even though she could tell

Dr. Wardman was using the striptease to hold the bad guys' attention.

Then all hell broke loose; she saw two of the gunmen go down. Then there were three bodies lying on the floor, covered by sheets, one of them in the corner away from the entrance to the room.

"You got all of them?" she asked.

"Yes," Grant answered.

His tone was firm, but she was having trouble believing him.

"I only saw two get shot," she said, hearing the strained quality of her own voice. "And when you got me from the car, I only saw two bodies."

Before Grant could answer, Mack jumped in. "That's because of the camera angles. He was in a blind spot. And he fell far back in the room where you couldn't see him."

"Okay," she answered, wishing she could have seen the third guy go down. He was the one she feared the most, but she wasn't going to talk about any of that.

"So you don't have to run away again," Grant said.

Her head swung toward him, her gaze questioning.

"None of them will be coming back to get you."

She nodded slowly, still trying to absorb the impact and the implications.

"We're going to go on with business as usual," Grant said. "The patients will be moved back to the regular-care facility as soon as we get it back in shape."

Lily turned toward her. "Mack is the only patient before you who came out of the VR. He had to get into reasonable shape quickly because we were under attack. But you have the luxury of easing back into the real world."

"I guess."

"I'd like you to stay at a nearby Decorah safe house," she said.

"Why do I need to be at a safe house?"

"You don't. Not strictly speaking. But we're being cautious. Plus it's got a gym, a running trail, a gourmet kitchen, access to every news and entertainment outlet. Anything you want. It's a good place for you to get used to regular living. And while you're there, you may be able to help us find Gabe Thompson."

Grant stood up, walked down the hall and came back. "It's dark outside. I'd like to get you settled at the safe house."

"Okay," she answered, thinking that he and Lily were very effectively boxing her in.

When he dragged in a breath and let it out, she wondered what he didn't want to say. "I'm sure that nobody knows you're here. But I'm not going to take any chances either. We're going to leave in Mack and Lily's car. And you're going to be dressed like Lily. If anyone is watching, they'll think you're her—and I'm Mack"

"How could they be watching?" Jenny asked.

"It would have to be from a distance, and I don't think they are, but I'm not taking any chances," Grant answered. "I asked Lily to go out earlier and bring back takeout for lunch. She left the clothing she was wearing in a bag in the closet where you were sleeping. Put the outfit on, and also put on the wig I left. You already look a lot like her, but that will clinch it.

"And what happens when Lily really leaves?"

"She's going to be wheeled out and put into an ambulance," Frank answered. "Anybody watching will think she's one of the patients—having some kind of crisis."

"Okay, yes, but what if they follow the ambulance to the hospital?"

"By that time, it won't matter," Mack answered. "Or—if they do, they'll realize they've been tricked. Grant's going to take my car and drive to the safe house later. Then we'll switch."

* * *

Carlos Mardano and another one of Rambo's security men, a guy named Tino Barcan, had made themselves at home in the parking lot of a strip mall conveniently situated across the highway from the entrance to the industrial park where the Decorah offices were located. They had driven down from New Jersey together. When they'd arrived in the Baltimore-Washington area, they had rented several cars so that they could rotate the vehicles to keep from being too conspicuous in their spy activities.

Carlos was getting tired of eating hamburgers and fries, but from his vantage point across the highway, he was sure he could figure out what was going on with Decorah.

This evening they each sat in a separate car and had taken turns going into the fast-food restaurant in the mall for coffee and sandwiches and to use the john. The arrangement meant that one of them was always monitoring the traffic going in and out of the park.

He had spun the story of the attack at the medical facility to his advantage, and he'd escaped with his life—unlike Danny and Lee, who had been killed in the shoot-out. He'd also told Rambo that he was going to bring Jenny back. And now he had to deliver.

The night after the failed attempt to scoop her up, he'd been able to take a look at the scene of the carnage by going in through the woods that bordered the industrial park. It was clear that the Decorah guys weren't going to be using the location until it was cleaned up. So he'd abandoned his plans to focus on that place and gone searching for the main Decorah office. It wasn't hard to find. Decorah was a private security agency located a few miles down the road from the place where they'd housed all the sleepers. It looked like the patients who had been lying there during the search for Jenny were at the other building now. And probably, Jenny, too, if he was right about the doctor lying.

So why was a security agency running a hospital for brain-injured patients? He did some research on the Web and found that Decorah was involved in a fair amount of charity work. Maybe that was why they were housing a bunch of people who might never recover.

But Jenny hadn't been lying in one of those beds. Either she was ambulatory, or she was dead. And from the way that doctor had acted, he was betting on the former.

With no choice, Jenny stood up and walked down the hall, wondering what the others were going to say after she left. Or maybe they wouldn't take a chance on discussing the case until she was out of the building.

Was there a back way out of here? Even if there was, it wouldn't do her any good. Trying to get away with so many Decorah agents in the building—plus Frank Decorah himself—wouldn't be smart.

Instead she walked into the room where she'd been asleep and opened the closet. The paper bag she hadn't noticed before was on the floor. Opening it, she took out a lime-green blouse, navy slacks and a short dark wig.

As she picked up the blouse, she was thinking that it would show up pretty well in the dark. But that must have been what Grant had intended.

After putting on the blouse and slacks, she took the wig into the bathroom, where she tugged it into place and tucked her hair out of sight.

As she put on the blouse, she was thinking about the video the agents had made her view. She'd struggled not to be sick when she'd watched the invaders intimidate Lily and the other Decorah people. But seeing the bad guys dead had been a relief—although she couldn't push away a feeling of unreality about the takedown. The gruesome thought crossed her mind that she wished she'd seen their faces after they'd been shot. That would have made it real. And now it was too late to see the evidence.

CHAPTER FIFTEEN

A noise in the doorway made Jenny turn quickly. Grant was standing there, his gaze fixed on her.

"Are you all right?" he asked.

"Yes," she answered, trying to read his expression. They'd gotten very close while she was in the VR. She'd ruined that by running away, and she felt her insides clench when she thought about what might have been.

Then she swept that longing away. She had no business dragging a good man like Grant into the muck with her.

As he studied her, she wondered what he was thinking.

"You look a lot like Lily," he finally said.

"And you look a lot like Mack. That's convenient," she countered, turning the conversation away from herself.

He laughed. "Right. Exactly like Mack."

She turned back to the mirror to have one last look at the wig.

"We should get going."

"Uh huh." With no real alternative, she turned and followed him toward the front of the building.

He held her back as an ambulance drew up at the entrance. Medics rushed into the building rolling a stretcher between them. They moved into the lounge, where Lily was waiting, her hand clasped with Mack's. He helped her onto the stretcher, and the medics covered her body with a sheet that came up to her mouth. Next they draped a towel over the top of her head so that hardly any of her face was visible.

When she was ready, they wheeled her out, with Mack sticking close to her side. As soon as the doors closed, they pulled away sirens blaring.

Grant gave them a few minutes to clear the industrial park. Then he motioned to Jenny. "Come on. Let's get the hell out of here while the getting's good."

She followed him to the car and climbed in quickly, her mind scrambling for a way to get out of the mess she had created, because she knew they were going to check out her story. And they'd find some big holes. The only alternative she could think of was the one she had used earlier, only she was going to have to be a lot cleverer.

Carlos had seen an ambulance speed up the road to the Decorah office. Either one of the sleepers was sick, or something else was going on. Were they transferring Jenny? Or was that what they wanted anyone who was watching to think?

He was still considering his options when he saw a Decorah car coming down the access road. From the license, he could see it was the car that belonged to one of the Bradley brothers. Mack and Grant. Mack, the guy who had pretended to be an innocent bystander, was married to the doctor who had been so rudely interrupted doing her striptease. And the other was single—and maybe involved with Jenny Seaver, Carlos was guessing.

The car paused at the stop sign, waiting for traffic to clear on the highway. The couple inside looked like Lily Wardman and Mack Bradley, but Carlos had a funny feeling about the setup.

He called Tino on his cell.

"You follow that ambulance and find out what's going on. I'm going after the car that just made a right."

* * *

Despite using the ruse of the ambulance, Grant was alert for anyone following as he turned onto the highway and headed for the Decorah safe house. Once he imagined he saw a silver midsize sedan following, but it zipped past and disappeared into traffic.

Jenny was watching him. "What?"

"I thought I saw someone tailing me. But it passed us."

She craned her neck, looking through the windshield, but saw nothing.

The cars ahead of him slowed, and he hit the brake.

"An accident?" she asked.

"I hope it's just a slow down."

He shifted in his seat, impatient to get off the road and get Jenny to a safe place. But there was no way around the traffic that crept inch by inch along the highway.

An ambulance came speeding along the shoulder—presumably not the same ambulance that had carried Lily to the hospital.

Jenny glanced at him. She looked like she wanted to say something, but she didn't speak.

He was tempted to ask what she was thinking, but he didn't press her, partly because he wasn't sure how to respond.

He was going to protect her. But he was having trouble picturing a relationship with her. He'd thought she trusted him. More importantly, he'd thought he trusted her. Obviously neither of those things was true anymore. And now he was going off to be locked in a safe house with her until the Decorah team determined she was no longer in danger. He was hoping they could do it quickly. And then maybe they could talk—and she would tell him the things she was still holding back. She'd let him wonder if she'd been raped. But was that even true? Or had she seen an opportunity to keep him at arm's length?

120

After the initial traffic slow down, it was another twenty minutes before he drove past a three-car wreck. Then he was able to speed up again.

Once he was moving along on the highway, he looked around for the silver car he'd spotted. He thought he might have seen a similar vehicle, but then it was gone again.

He took a couple of turns, making sure he didn't take the direct route to the safe house. But finally he pulled up at the gate in the fence that encircled the wooded property.

After putting his key card into the slot, he pressed a code on the keypad. When the gate opened, he drove through and waited for the barrier to close behind him before he started up the winding drive toward the dwelling.

Floodlights came on as they approached what looked like a typical Maryland farmhouse.

They both climbed out of the car and walked up a couple of stairs to the front porch. When Jenny stepped inside, she stopped short as she looked around at the interior. The first floor had been completely transformed into a great room with a modern white eat-in kitchen taking up one quarter of the space and a comfortable lounge area occupying most of the rest.

"Nice," she murmured.

"There's a gym downstairs and a shooting range."

"Really?"

"All the comforts of home. And there's a safe room that's invasion proof, in case of trouble."

"But you're not expecting any."

"Correct," he agreed, then continued, "We have three bedrooms and three baths upstairs. The first room on the right is yours. There's clothing in the closet and in the dresser. I'll be at the other end of the hall. You can go up and relax, if you want. Or you can take a tour of the kitchen."

He watched her weighing her options. "Maybe I'll go up."

"Sure."

When she was gone, he looked to see what the team had put in the pantry and the refrigerator. Then he checked his e-mail to find out what Teddy had turned up on the mysterious Rambo or Gabe Thompson.

Carlos had stayed well back as he followed the Decorah car. He was in the white car that Tino had been driving earlier.

He and the other security man had changed cars a half hour earlier—after he had woven through traffic, causing the three-car accident on the highway, before speeding away.

As he'd anticipated, the accident had slowed the Decorah guy down considerably, giving Carlos a chance to get into position behind him again—then trade off with Tino so that neither one of them was following the whole time.

He'd hatched the plan after Tino had called to report that the ambulance was a decoy. The lady doctor had emerged from the emergency room entrance ten minutes after the ambulance had taken the "patient" in. And one of the Bradley brother had met her. They'd hugged and driven off together.

All that led to the further conclusion that the couple in the car were Jenny Seaver, disguised as Lily Wardman, and the other Bradley brother—Grant. That all sounded hard to follow, but it was really pretty simply. They'd used the ambulance as a decoy to spirit Jenny away, and he'd hustled to get on top of the deception. Plus now he knew where the little bitch was hiding. She couldn't stay in there forever. And maybe there was even a way to persuade her to come out. If not that, maybe he could lure out the guy who was guarding her. Grant Bradley.

He'd have to think about those tactics. For the time being, he was content to know that he hadn't lost Jenny Seaver.

* * *

Jenny opened the door and walked into the first room on the right. It was clear immediately that it had been decorated for female guests. There was a four-poster double bed that looked like mahogany, a matching dresser and mirror, a muted Oriental rug on the polished wood floor, and a small padded rocking chair in one corner. The bathroom wasn't large, but it had been nicely outfitted with a small marble-topped vanity, a shower and one of those modern toilets that lets you use it like a bidet.

One wall of the bedroom was taken up by a closet with apparel that seemed to be her size. As she looked through the clothing, she saw jeans, less casual slacks, shirts and tees, plus running shoes, heels and flats. It appeared that someone had gone to a lot of trouble to give her a wardrobe. Had Grant bought all that? And what was he assuming about how long she'd be here?

The last thought was unsettling. Decorah might think she was going to be safe, but she doubted it—even with the men who had invaded the patient facility eliminated. Rambo would figure out where she was again and send more goons.

She glanced over her shoulder, then turned on the light and closed the bedroom door. Next she glanced toward the window, wondering if anyone could see her from outside. Quickly she closed the blinds, trying to convince herself that she felt safe.

As she paced the room, she thought back over the way the Decorah agents had acted when they'd interviewed her and shown her the video. She was sure they were keeping something from her, but she had no idea what it was.

She let the inevitable conclusion of that scenario play through her mind and shuddered. But she couldn't deal with it now. And she was dead tired. Which was weird because she'd had a nice long sleep a few hours ago, courtesy of the drug Dr. Wardman had given her.

Once again she glanced toward the door, then began opening drawers in the dresser. She took out a pair of sweatpants, then grabbed a tee shirt from a hanger in the closet. She went into the bathroom to put them on, then climbed into bed, still worried about something she couldn't quite name. But she was too wrung out by everything that had happened to examine any problems now.

She couldn't help wishing she was back in the VR. She'd been safe there. No, that was just an illusion. She'd known all along that she couldn't stay. And she'd been right. Only hours after she'd left an invasion force had come to scoop her up. And what if they had caught up with her?

She shuddered. For now, she should stop torturing herself. She had to get some rest and then figure out what she was going to do in the morning.

She wondered if it was possible to sleep, but really she was so emotionally and physically exhausted that she dropped off quickly. And in her sleep, she got everything she wanted.

Against all odds, she was back in the VR, so happy to find herself in the familiar, calming environment. Coming in through the room Lily had set up as a transition for visitors, she knew at once where she was.

Raising her arm, she saw that she was wearing the running suit that she remembered from the first time she'd awakened here. Even the soft fabric against her skin was comforting. And with a feeling of relief, she stepped into the elegance of the lobby, breathing in the flower-scented air and looking around at the opulent surroundings. It was like coming home to be here again.

The women behind the desk looked up and smiled. "We missed you. Welcome back."

"Thanks. I missed being here," she answered with heartfelt honesty. How had she ever come up with the idea of leaving this peaceful place?

"Are you going to your room?" the desk attendant asked.

"I think I'll go down to the pool."

"Did you bring a suit?"

"I'll stop in the lobby shop."

With a sudden flood of energy, she strode across the marble floor and stepped into the small store, where she examined the swimming suits on shelves along one wall and snatched up one. With the scant garment clutched in her hand, she hurried out of the building and down the path to the pool complex.

Usually she might pass some of the other guests on her way. Paula could be out here painting. Or Shelly might be playing on the lawn, watched over by her nurse. But not today, and Jenny was glad that she was alone. She didn't want to see any of the people who lived here. There was only one person she wanted to meet.

Her heart beat faster as she descended the steps to the pool, her gaze sweeping over the sparkling blue of the water. The swimming complex was empty, and she hesitated for a moment. Was she wrong? Had she come here only to be disappointed?

Thrusting that worry aside, she hurried to the cabana where she and Grant had made love. After stepping inside, she started pulling off the running suit. When she was naked, she reached for the bathing suit, then tossed it onto the chair in the corner. Instead, she went to the hanging rack and took down one of the terry robes. Her heart was thumping as she shrugged into the robe and tied the belt. Once again she wondered, was she wrong about all this? Or ...

She didn't allow herself to finish the sentence as she stepped outside and scanned the pool area. Her heart leaped when she saw Grant coming down the steps. He was dressed in faded jeans, but that was all he was wearing. He was barefoot and shirtless, and his gaze fixed on her. He walked with deliberate purpose, each step bringing him closer to her.

She forgot to breathe as he stopped in front of her, only inches away, a question in his eyes.

"Grant," she breathed. "I wanted you here."

"I wasn't sure you did."

"Never doubt how much I want to be with you," she answered, hearing the slight quaver in her voice.

Every word she spoke was true. Forget that back in the real world, everything had been wrong between them. Here, everything could be right, because she was making the rules.

The thought gave her pause. Back in the real world?

He was watching her, and she knew that he wouldn't reach for her. She must be the one because she had to prove that her words of reassurance to him were true.

CHAPTER SIXTEEN

In the great room of the safe house, Grant tried to focus on the laptop computer screen, tried to read the information that Teddy Granada had sent him. But keeping his mind on work was impossible. All he could think about was the woman who had walked upstairs—the woman who had walked away from him a little while ago.

It was his own fault, he supposed. He'd practically pushed her away because no matter how much he wanted to protect her—and trust her and help her heal—he couldn't really let down his guard, not after all her deceptions. And he understood that it was because of his own fear that she could hurt him more than any other person in the world.

He knew that was true. But he was alone, and it was safe to admit how much he wanted her—and how much he wanted a future with her.

With a sigh, he set the computer on the side table, leaned back in the comfortable chair and closed his eyes, imagining that the two of them were together again in the VR, the way they had been the time he'd come down to the pool, and they'd made love. He'd been elated that she'd reached for him. Then the next day, she'd run away, and he'd known she was really saying good-bye.

He shoved that last part aside. She'd had her reasons for running, and he knew a big factor was her fear that he and the other Decorah people were in danger because of her.

But now it was like a miracle. They were back in the VR together, as though none of the bad stuff had happened. Not her running away. Not the shoot-out among the sleeping patients. Not her lies. And not his deception.

"*Grant, I wanted you here—so much,*" she murmured, and he also heard the words in his mind like when he and his brother communicated without speaking.

I wasn't sure you did.

Never doubt how much I want to be with you," she answered.

He had never encountered anything like this—but he let himself surrender to the experience, telling himself that he would deal with reality later. Right now, all he wanted was to get as close to this woman as he could.

Jenny shoved doubt away and reached for Grant, raising her arms so that she could cup the back of his head and bring his mouth to hers.

She felt instant heat—and relief—that the two of them could bridge the gap she had created by leaving the VR against doctor's orders.

She'd done it because all the bad stuff was her fault. Much as she wanted to deny it, she knew it was true.

As Grant's lips touched down on hers, he made a sound deep in his throat, a sound that told her he wanted this as much as she did.

And as he claimed her, he took the lead, moving his mouth against hers in nibbles and sweeping caresses and finally more intimately when she opened her mouth for him. Last time neither of them had known what to expect. This time each of them was sure of the other. And each of them knew how to give the other pleasure.

While he kissed her, he gathered her close, his hands moving over her back and shoulder and into her hair. She could feel his erection, hard and bold.

When she moved against it, he caught his breath.

"Don't. I want to go slow."

"How is that possible?"

She felt him grin. "Because I'm not going to make love with you until you're as hot as I am. Come inside."

She watched him grin again as he knitted his fingers with hers and led her through the curtains into the private cabana. Only it wasn't the cabana she had stepped out of a few minutes earlier.

It was totally transformed into a bedroom in a pleasure palace. The walls were draped with golden hangings. The floor under her bare feet was made of something soft that felt like a cross between plush carpet and well-tended lawn. And in the center of the room was a wide bed with embroidered pillows at the head and a silk coverlet.

"Did you do this?" she whispered.

"Yes. For you. I want everything to be perfect for you."

"I want everything to be perfect for you, too," she answered, then felt a dart of guilt. "What am I doing?" she asked in a small voice.

The expression of satisfaction disappeared from his face. "You don't want to be with me?"

"Of course I do. But I'm making this up. It's not real."

"Yes it is."

"But it's only my dream."

"No. It's my dream too," he answered, his voice firm.

She stared at him in disbelief. "How?"

"I don't know. But I know it's real. I'm here with you. Back there, we were uncomfortable with each other. I didn't know how I was going to spend time at the safe house alone with you. And I think you felt the same. Neither one of us could admit how much we wanted each other in real life. But we can admit it here."

"Lord, yes," she breathed, so thankful that she wasn't just giving herself forbidden pleasure.

He fumbled for the belt of the robe, opening the tie and sweeping the edges of the garment out of the way.

She'd deliberately worn nothing underneath, but now she felt exposed as he took a step back and looked at her.

"Beautiful."

"I want to be—for you," she said, admitting what she couldn't say in reality.

"You're perfect."

He reached for her, running his fingers down her sides and over her hips, and the feel of his large hands on her naked body sent a shock wave through her.

He brought his hands inward, moving to her stomach and playing with her navel before reaching to cup her breasts.

She heard a needy sound escape her lips as he took her breasts in his hands, and her need redoubled as he stroked his thumbs across nipples that had hardened to tight points of sensation.

When she felt him go still, she raised her head, giving him a questioning look.

"Are you sure you want to do this?" he asked in a gritty voice.

"Would we be here together if both of us didn't want this?" she countered.

"Good point."

Her gaze locked with his, she shrugged her shoulders out of the robe, letting it fall to the floor as she reached for his belt buckle and opened it before finding the metal button at the top of his jeans.

She kept her gaze on his face as she lowered the zipper. Both of them held their breath as she reached inside. She'd expected to encounter his shorts. But just as she'd worn nothing under her robe, he was naked under his jeans.

"Oh."

"I guess we were both on the same wavelength."

"Convenient," she murmured, surprised by her own boldness.

He sucked in a sharp breath as she closed her fingers around his erection. "That's good. Probably too good."

"I want it to be good," she answered.

He threw his head back, enjoying her attentions for a few more moments before lifting her hand away, then used his feet to drag his jeans down before kicking them away.

Determined not to be shy, she reached around him, cupping his bottom, stroking and kneading her hands over his warm skin.

"That's nice." He did the same for her, but after gliding his hands over her bottom, he reached lower into the folds of her sex, caressing her there with knowing fingers.

"Oh, Lord," she managed to say, her voice sounding almost like a moan.

His other hand went back to her breasts, squeezing and tugging on her nipples.

"I don't think I can stand up much longer," she whispered.

"Me neither."

With the sumptuous bed only steps away, he lifted her up and carried her over, laying her on the horizontal surface. He looked magnificent standing over her.

He joined her on the bed, gathering her close, holding her for long moments as he brought his mouth back to hers.

They exchanged greedy kisses before his mouth moved to her ear, where he sucked on her lobe, then trailed his lips down to her neck and lower.

When he buried his face between her breasts, she clasped the back of his head.

He turned to the side, finding one nipple with his tongue, then moving so he could suck her into his mouth while his hand trailed down her body and into her slick folds.

As he stroked her there, she thought she would go up in flames.

"Don't make me wait," she pleaded.

He lifted his head so that he could speak. "I want you as hot as I am."

"I am!"

"We'll see."

When he dipped into her vagina, she felt her muscles ripple around his finger. He gave her a knowing look, then trailed moisture up and around her clit, and she knew she couldn't take much more.

Sliding her hand down his body, she caught his erection in her fist, squeezing and releasing, feeling the heat and power of him.

He gasped out her name.

"Do it now," she answered, rolling to her back and opening her legs for him.

He knelt in the V of her thighs, then angled his body so that the tip of his penis probed her opening. And then he was inside.

"I'm so glad you're here," she breathed.

"Oh yeah."

When he began to move, she matched his rhythm, knowing he was holding back, waiting for her to catch up with him. She was so hot that she climbed quickly to his level where she was helpless to do anything besides drive for her satisfaction.

She climaxed in a burst of ecstasy that carried her into space.

She knew he was with her as she felt his body go rigid, and heard his shout of satisfaction.

His weight pressed against her until he rolled to his side, gathering her to him, his breath still coming fast and hard.

"Thank you for this," he murmured.

"At first, I thought I had only imagined I was with you."

"No. You brought me here," he answered, his voice ringing with conviction.

The declaration was comforting, yet she had to ask, "Now what?"

The question hung in the air between them. They'd both done what they desperately wanted to do, what neither of them could have admitted at the safe house. But they'd come together in this place that was beyond the realm of ordinary life. Really, it was beyond her previous experience. She's been in the VR. And she'd been in the real world. This was neither. And she wanted to stay here with Grant.

The concept was tempting, yet she knew that it was outside the laws of time and space. She could pretend they were safe, but that only increased the danger for both of them.

The insight made her clasp Grant more tightly, and in turn, he gathered her closer.

She snuggled against him, so glad to be in his arms like this.

"Thank you," she murmured.

"I think you had a lot to do with the great sex."

She flushed. "Well, I was thanking you for coming here."

"You called out to me."

"How?"

"I don't exactly know. Like I said, maybe I could hear you because of the way my brother and I communicate mind to mind."

"But you don't have a mental experience where you step into the same location?"

Never. We just have conversations in our heads that nobody else can hear."

"And how do you start the conversation?"

"One of us 'calls' the other. Kind of like you called me."

"But I didn't know I was doing it."

He shrugged. "It worked."

"Did it really?" she asked.

CHAPTER SEVENTEEN

As Jenny asked the question, everything around her changed. One moment she was in Grant's arms. In the next heartbeat, she was back in the guest room of the safe house.

She had been on her side, snuggled against Grant. In reality, she lay on her back with the covers tangled around her legs and her hand down the front of her sweatpants. She quickly pulled it out and lay with her breath coming fast, still awash in sexual satisfaction.

In the VR? No in her very own fantasy VR, where she'd been talking urgently to Grant, trying to reassure herself that he'd really been with her there and that the pleasure she'd experienced hadn't been hers alone.

He'd told her he was with her, feeling the same things she was feeling. And of course he would say that in *her* fantasy. Yet the hand between her legs told her that she'd been the one to bring herself to climax. At least as far as reality was concerned.

The idea of facing Grant now made her face heat as it had a few moments ago in her dream encounter. Yet she couldn't simply leave the all-important question hanging in her mind. Had he really been there making love with her?

Turning her head, she glanced at the clock on the bedside table. It was four in the morning. Was Grant still downstairs? Or was she going to have to knock on his bedroom door?

Her mouth twisted into a grimace as she climbed out of bed, straightened her clothing, and headed for the door.

She didn't want to face Grant now. Yet she knew honesty required her to do it.

Gripping the banister, she made her way down the steps, then into the great room. Grant was standing beside the easy chair, his gaze riveted to her. The moment she saw his face, she knew she hadn't been conjuring up reassurances to make herself feel better. He had been in the fantasy VR with her.

She walked straight into his arms, and he clasped her to him, the way he had done when they'd been lying in that fancy bedroom a few minutes earlier.

Her arms tightened around him. "It was real," she whispered.

"Sort of real."

"I mean, we were together. It wasn't just me, conjuring up a Grant simulacrum, like the woman who works behind the desk at the Mirador. Or the nurse who takes care of Shelly."

"No. It was me—making love with you," he said, his voice edgy and his meaning very clear.

She nodded against his shoulder. "I wanted you so much."

"I wanted you too, but it seems neither one of us could admit it. We were each clutching at the reasons why we had to stay apart."

But she could still feel her own uncertainty as they held each other.

"You put me in a guest room," she said in a barely audible voice. "You should come up to bed with me now."

"That's what you want?"

"Yes."

He clasped his hand with hers, and they climbed the steps to the second floor, where they walked into the room she'd just left.

When he looked at the bed, she flushed. "I guess I was pretty ... restless."

"Uh huh."

He turned to her again, and they came together for a long sweet kiss.

Kissing and touching, they slowly undressed each other, then climbed into the bed. As they made love all over again, she savored every precious moment of the encounter. She wanted to be with this man—so much, even though she was still the woman who could bring down death and destruction on him and all of his friends.

But they were here together now. And she wouldn't deny herself anything she could gather up from these precious moments with him.

"Our first time together," she whispered as she lay in his arms in the aftermath.

"Yeah." He settled her more comfortably against himself, and she nestled down to sleep beside him—overwhelmed by the luxury of the whole experience. When she reached for his hand, he wove his fingers with hers.

They could be a married couple, sleeping beside each other as they did every night of their lives. But they weren't any kind of married couple, and sleeping beside Grant was a rare joy.

Questions were still swirling in her mind. But she wouldn't spoil this moment by asking them. Not yet.

Grant woke early and turned his head, looking at the woman lying next to him. Making love with her had been fantastic—just as good in the real world as in the fantasy version of the VR.

Still, he didn't trust Jenny any more than he would trust a sideshow barker touting the wonders of the exhibits inside the tent behind him.

He wanted to wake her up. Maybe in that moment when she was caught off guard, she'd tell him why she was still hiding something important from him.

Instead he eased out of bed, scooped up the clothing he'd discarded on the floor, and headed down the hall to his own room. After showering and dressing he went downstairs to the computer and scanned the e-mail from Decorah Security.

Using high tech equipment, Lily had been able to sequence the DNA from the two dead men. And Teddy used the information when he'd tapped into a government database.

It turned out that both men were petty criminals from New Jersey, which at least backed up the story about where Jenny was from. But that was as much as they'd been able to glean.

Grant made a low sound. Too bad he couldn't talk about the results with Jenny. But if he did, he'd have to lie and say they had DNA from three dead guys—instead of the two actual bodies.

But he was sure the dead men weren't the key to finding out what Jenny was hiding. It was the woman herself—if she'd only trust him enough to tell him what was going on. Which gave him an idea he hadn't considered earlier. They'd taken DNA from the dead men, but they hadn't tested Jenny. Suppose he got DNA from her? Would that tell them who she really was?

He sent a message to Lily.

"What if we test Jenny's DNA?"

"Good idea. How do we get a sample?" she asked.

"I can get it at breakfast. But then what?"

"I can send a messenger over."

"We'd better have a cover story for why he's coming."

"I decided she should be having protein shakes?"

"Okay."

With the plan in place, he turned in a status report on the time since he'd left the Decorah patient facility—leaving out all of the personal stuff. He debated telling Mack about establishing a telepathic link with Jenny, then decided it was prudent to include the information. Hopefully, he wouldn't have to explain how they'd done it. He didn't want to have a big discussion about that now.

After sending the message, he walked into the kitchen and checked out the supplies. In his family, the men had been as good with a skillet and spatula as the women. And the least he could do for Jenny was make her a good breakfast. The trouble was, he didn't want to do the least. He wanted to do the most—if she would only let him.

Jenny woke much later than she expected and found that Grant had already gotten up—but let her sleep.

After a quick shower, she pulled on jeans and a knit top, then hesitated for a few moments. There was something she wanted to ask him, but was it a good idea to bring up— business?

Well, maybe there was no way around it, she told herself as she exited the bedroom.

She was still focused on the problem as she walked down the hall. But as she descended the stairs, delicious aromas wafted up toward her, making her stomach growl, and she realized that she'd eaten almost nothing in twenty-four hours.

When she walked into the kitchen, Grant was standing at the stove frying French toast. He kept his gaze focused on the skillet, making her wonder if he was having a similar problem to hers. Was there something he didn't want to talk about— but felt was necessary?

Focusing on the food, she crossed the floor and picked up one of the pieces of bacon he'd fried.

"This is good."

"Thanks."

"I should be doing the cooking," she said.

"Why?"

"It's the woman's job."

He turned to her. "What would you have cooked if I hadn't started breakfast?"

She looked at what he'd produced. "Probably burned toast and overdone scrambled eggs."

When he raised an eyebrow, she admitted, "I don't actually know a lot about cooking."

"You had a maid when you were a kid?"

"Yes. And later, too." she said in a low voice, hoping she had made it clear that she didn't want to talk about her background.

He gave her a quick look, then got down plates from the cabinet.

"Help yourself."

She took another strip of bacon and two pieces of French toast, then poured on some of the syrup that was sitting on the counter.

"Coffee?"

"Yes," she answered, thinking that this was another milestone—their first meal together. But how many more would there be?

They took seats across from each other. Focusing on her plate, she used her fork to cut the French toast and took a bite.

"Really good."

"My dad taught me to make it."

"What did he do? I mean his job."

"He was an outfitter in Western Maryland."

Glad to keep the conversation's focus off herself, she asked, "What exactly is an outfitter? He made clothing?"

Grant laughed. "No, he took people on outdoor expeditions. Like rock climbing, whitewater rafting, camping in the wilderness. Exploring natural caves. And when my brother and I got old enough, we sometimes went along."

"Sounds wonderful."

"You never did anything like that? I had friends whose sisters were Girl Scouts, and they got to go camping."

"No, I was expected to be a perfect little lady."

"Okay."

She cut off a piece of French toast and pushed it around her plate, thinking it was better to shift away from herself, even if she didn't exactly like the topic."

"I wanted to ask you about that video you showed me yesterday."

His head jerked up. "What about it?"

"Can I see it again?"

His voice took on a sharp edge. "Why?"

She picked her words carefully. "Maybe if I look at it, I can help you with some more information. Do you have a copy of the tape?"

"Yes. Maybe after breakfast we could look at it."

"Thanks," she said and went back to eating the meal he had prepared, although her appetite had diminished considerably. Afterwards she cleared the table, then opened the dishwasher, looking at the spokes inside and wondering exactly how to put the dishes in. She decided the plates should line up in rows and the cups should be in the top. When she turned around, she saw Grant watching her.

"You turn the cups upside down," he said.

She flushed as she stared at the china she'd put into the machine. "Right. That would make sense."

"You never loaded a dishwasher?"

She shook her head. "I guess I was a rich little girl princess."

"What did your father do?"

"Import, export," she answered quickly.

Grant didn't reply as he turned over the cups.

She didn't want to ask about the video again, but he brought it up when the kitchen was clean.

"We can watch the surveillance tape."

"Thanks."

"Go on into the great room, and I'll be right there."

She went to the sitting area and settled on the sofa. After a few moments, he joined her and retrieved a file from the laptop. Staring at the screen, she watched the familiar scene unfold. First she saw Lily and her orderly, Terry, in the patient facility. Then two tough-looking men came in and held them at gunpoint. A third man marched Mack in, and things went downhill from there.

As the events unfolded, she kept an eye on the time stamp in the upper right hand corner of the screen. At first it flowed along with no interruptions. But near the end, when she saw the bodies under sheets on the floor, there was a jump in the time.

She sat very still, struggling not to react to what she had just seen.

Grant's voice startled her. "Did you find anything we can use?"

"No, sorry," she answered, managing to keep her voice steady.

Leaning back against the cushions, she made a small sound.

"What?"

"That was upsetting."

"Yeah."

"You know I feel guilty about bringing this down on all of you."

"It's not your fault," he repeated what he'd said earlier.

"Technically."

She turned her head away, thinking there was more than one technicality involved here. Really, she wanted to get away from Grant and be on her own to think about what she'd just discovered. But she didn't know how to manage it.

She had been going to say she was still not up to par physically and needed to take a nap when a buzzer startled her.

"What was that?"

141

"The front gate."

He used the computer to bring up the image of a man leaning out of a car window.

"Yes?"

"I have the protein shakes Dr. Wardman ordered for Ms. Seaver."

Jenny stared at the image. "I'm getting protein shakes?"

"Yeah."

Grant buzzed the man in, and a minute later a car arrived in front of the house. When Jenny started toward the door, Grant stopped her.

"Let me."

He walked into the kitchen and picked up an envelope.

"What's that?" she asked.

"Grocery list."

He took the envelope out and returned a few minutes later with a bag of powdered shake packets.

"Maybe you should have one," he said.

"Sure."

He took the bag into the kitchen and began preparing a shake.

"You're sure it's not some kind of—medicine?"

"I don't think so."

After making the shake, he poured two glasses. They each took one and sipped, but she couldn't help thinking he was acting strange. All the more reason to implement the plan that was starting to form in her mind.

When she'd finished her shake, she put down her glass and said, "You mentioned there was a shooting range and a gym."

"In the basement."

"Maybe working out would be a good idea."

"Okay," he answered, and from the way he said it, she wondered if he had been thinking of other ways to pass the time. Like making love, for example. Could she do that, after what she'd seen on the video?

"Show me what you have in the gym," she said.

"Sure. We could both change, and work out."

So he wasn't planning to leave her alone. What did he think she was going to do—run out of the house and try to get away? Once again, she struggled not to reveal her emotions.

"Okay."

They each went to their own bedroom. She found shorts, a tee shirt and running shoes in the closet and pulled them on. When she came downstairs again, she saw that Grant was similarly dressed. Only her tee shirt was plain white and his said Decorah Security.

He opened the basement door, and they went down the stairs, descending to a hallway that led to several rooms.

"While we're down here, I should show you the safe room I told you about."

"Oh, right."

He opened a door to his immediate right, and she saw a room that looked like it was equipped for a siege with bunk beds, canned and dried food, chemical toilets and communications equipment.

"If something happens to me, you go right down here and lock the door. Then call Decorah."

"What would happen to you?"

"I think we're safe here, but I want you prepared for anything."

"Okay, then can you tell where I can get a weapon if I need it."

"There are automatic pistols upstairs in the cabinet near the door. And down here there are also automatic rifles in the gun cabinet. But I hope you're not going to need them."

She nodded, thinking she hoped so, too. At least not here.

CHAPTER EIGHTEEN

Jenny followed Grant along on his tour of the facility.

Next he showed her the shooting range. And finally they stepped into a very well equipped gym.

There was one bike and one treadmill, at opposite ends of the room. After taking in the layout, she said, "I'm going to warm up on the stationary bike. Then I'll do some of the weight machines."

"Okay. I'll start on the treadmill."

Seated on the bike, she set the program for a random pattern and began to pedal, keeping her gaze focused on the screen which showed a forest and then a mountain scene as she began to climb a hill.

She pumped the pedals at a vigorous pace. Along with her legs, her mind was racing as she went back to what she'd seen on the video. The gaps in the time stamp meant that the Decorah people had stopped the tape and started it again. And she had a pretty good guess about why.

She had seen two of the invaders go down. That was a definite. Later she had seen three bodies, and they had claimed the camera angle was wrong to show the third man getting hit. She'd been thrown off balance by having to face the action the first time. Yet something about the tape had nagged at her. Now she suspected why she hadn't seen the third man get shot—because he'd gotten away.

She shuddered. The two who had died were hired thugs she didn't recognize. The third one was a guy named Carlos she had seen many times. Surely he was the leader of the trio. They hadn't been able to show her his body because there *was* no body. The most dangerous man in the trio had escaped. So they'd faked it. She could be wrong about the man who had gotten away, but she didn't think so.

Why had the Decorah agents set up the false narrative?

She had an answer for that too. They wanted to make her feel safer because all the men who had tracked her to Decorah were dead. That way, she would go along with their plan of stashing her here while they dug into her background and tried to figure out what she was hiding.

She glanced up at Grant who was running on the treadmill. Before he could see her watching him, she lowered her gaze again to the screen in front of her. She supposed there was some chance that the doctored tape was meant to fool him, too. But she had trouble believing that. Maybe he had even been the one to come up with the idea. For her own good, as far as they were concerned.

She clenched her hands around the grips of the bike and clenched her teeth to keep herself from screaming from across the room that she'd figured out their dirty little secret.

She wanted to explain to Grant that Carlos was a dangerous man. But if she said that, she'd have to explain how she knew. And she obviously wasn't going to get into that.

The only thing she had going for her now was that Decorah had kept Carlos from following Grant and discovering this location. She was safe for now, but Lord knew what the man would do if he figured out where she was.

She meant—what he'd do to her. And then what he'd do to Decorah Security because he worked for Rambo—a relentless bastard who would go after the whole organization with a vengeance.

145

She closed her eyes for a moment, struggling with her altered situation. Or to be more precise—a reality that hadn't changed since she'd stolen a car three months ago and fled.

Rambo would keep looking for her. Keep coming after her. And there was only one way to change that equation. When she'd run away, she'd thought that would be enough. She'd found out she had underestimated the situation.

Did she have the guts to put the danger to rest once and for all? Did she have the guts to do it even if she might not survive? And if she did survive, then she'd have to disappear forever.

She swallowed hard. This morning in the kitchen, she'd gotten a lesson in how ill equipped she was for life on her own.

But she was smart, and she was a fast learner. Her defensive training in the VR had taught her that.

The bike started up another steep incline, and she kept peddling furiously.

This time she was going to have to be a lot smarter if she wanted to get away from Grant, because he was on alert—waiting for her to try something.

They spent an hour in the gym, both of them slick with sweat when they finished their workouts.

She went up to her bathroom, but before she took a shower, she looked in the medicine cabinet. To her surprise, she found something very useful—a bottle of prescription sleeping pills. If she could get one of them into Grant's food or drink, that would give her the chance she needed to escape.

But he had to think that everything was okay with her now—and okay between them. Which meant she'd have to act perfectly normally when she met him again in the great room.

A half hour later, when she came downstairs, she saw that Grant had also showered and changed into jeans and a dark tee shirt. He looked so appealing that the sight of him made her catch her breath. He was typing on his laptop which he closed up when he saw her approaching.

"Working?" she asked, trying to keep any hint of disapproval out of her voice.

"Checking out some stuff with Decorah."

"Like what?"

He lifted his gaze, focusing on her face. "We have a line on Rambo."

As she heard the words, she felt a cold shiver go down her spine. "You do?"

"Yes. You said the guy who kidnapped you was a relatively young man?"

"Yes."

"The guy named Rambo has been around for a while. He's probably in his sixties."

Her mouth was so dry she could hardly speak. "Do you have his name?"

"Not yet, but Teddy is working on it."

Which meant maybe she had to move up her timetable. She'd thought she could wait till evening before she made her escape. Now it looked like she had to get out of here as soon as possible.

"Maybe you could give me a cooking lesson at lunch."

He laughed. "Changing the subject?"

"Yes, but it looks like I could use some life skills."

"Okay. What do you want to cook?"

"What do you want for lunch?"

He thought for a moment. "How about mac and cheese?"

"Oh, I like that. Is it hard to make?"

"Not really. Let's see if we have the ingredients."

"Okay. I'll be right back. I want to go upstairs for a minute first."

Grant watched Jenny climb the stairs, one hand on the banister. She was up to something, and he'd like to know

147

what, although he thought he had a pretty good idea. She was trying to act casually, but she'd been jumpy as a cat on a kitchen counter ever since she'd watched the video this morning. Either the whole captive shoot-out scene had upset her, or she'd picked up on the little alteration they'd made in the tape. Which meant he'd better stay on the alert.

She disappeared from view, and he thought about when they'd been cleaning up after breakfast. She hadn't known which way to put the cups in the dishwasher.

What kind of woman didn't know that? The only answer was—one who had no idea how a kitchen functioned. From her reaction to the Mirador hotel, he'd concluded that she came from a privileged background. He simply hadn't been prepared for how privileged.

What would it be like to marry someone who was so unprepared for life in the world?

Marry? That verb stopped him short. Was he thinking about marrying her?

Yeah, he knew he was thinking about it, despite all the reasons why it was a crazy idea. Starting with the little problem that they still didn't trust each other. And proceeding to the admission that he really knew very little about her.

But maybe she'd open up with him—after this mess was over.

Upstairs, Jenny walked into her bedroom, where she got out the bottle of sleeping pills. After shaking out two onto the bathroom counter, she used the bottom of a glass to crush them. Then she scooped the powder into a tissue, folded it closed and tucked it into the pocket of her jeans. To make it look like she'd really had a reason to go up, she flushed the toilet and washed her hands.

Downstairs, when Grant looked up as she came back to the kitchen area, she struggled not to seem on edge.

He went back to assembling the ingredients they'd need for lunch.

"First I'm going to boil some penne pasta," he said.

"I've only seen it made with elbow macaroni."

"Yes, but we don't have any, so we'll use what we've got."

The water was already boiling, and he put the pasta in, stirred it and lowered the heat a little. "You cook it uncovered. While it's cooking we'll make the sauce. I guess you don't know how to make a cheese sauce."

"Not a clue." She cleared her throat. "Could we have some wine with lunch?"

"Sure. There's some in the liquor cabinet in the great room. Get a nice bottle of red."

She found the cabinet and brought a bottle back to the kitchen, where he opened it.

"I'll pour," she offered.

While he ducked his head into the refrigerator for milk, butter, and cheese, she quickly dumped some of the sleeping powder into his wine, swirled it around, and set the glass near him.

As he turned back, she took a sip from her own glass. "Thanks for this. I think it will help me relax."

"Yeah," he answered, his voice sounding a little raw. He set a saucepan on the stove. "For this part, we're going to make a classic white sauce, then stir in cheese. First we melt some butter over medium heat. Then we stir in flour and finally milk. If you put the flour into cold milk, it will clump up."

"Okay."

He still hadn't touched his wine, but she wasn't going to press him to drink and make him wonder why she cared.

Instead she watched him do the things with the butter, flour and milk that he'd explained previously.

He'd already set a kind of pot with holes in the bottom in the sink, and when the timer rang for the pasta, he asked her to get a fork, take out a piece, blow on it to cool it, and see if it was done.

When she reported that it was, he carried the pot to the sink and emptied the contents into the thing with holes. The water ran out, and he transferred the pasta to a casserole dish.

Then he went back to the sauce. "Now for the cheese."

He took out a package of shredded cheddar and stirred some in. Then he got a spoon from the drawer and asked her to taste it.

"Enough cheese, do you think?"

"It's good. You really do know how to cook," she complimented him, feeling like she was a character in a play saying lines someone had fed her.

"Well, we'd better see how it all goes together." After pouring the cheese over the pasta and stirring it in, he tasted the results with the fork she'd used. "Okay, we could bake it to get it crusty on top, or we could just eat it this way."

"Let's eat now," she answered, anxious to get this over with.

He filled plates at the counter. They each picked up one, along with their wine and carried them to the table.

She tried not to look at his wine glass as he sat down.

Her appetite had completely gone, but she forced herself to fork up some of the dish he'd so expertly made.

"This is wonderful. Your mom taught you well."

He laughed. "Not Mom. This was one of Dad's specialties."

"Oh."

When he finally took a sip of wine, she held her breath, wondering if it was going to taste too bad for him to keep drinking it. But to her relief, he seemed to think it was okay and took another sip.

CHAPTER NINETEEN

For Jenny, trying to pretend this was simply a normal lunch felt like wading through a mud-sucking swamp. Probably the mac and cheese Grant had made was good, but she couldn't really taste it.

Several moments of silence passed while she thrashed around for something to talk about.

"So what are your favorite dishes?" he asked as he took another sip of wine.

That shouldn't be too hard to answer. "Um, I've always liked chicken."

"That's a pretty broad topic. Fried chicken?"

"No. Chicken cooked in sauce. Like chicken cacciatore or coq au vin."

"Mm." His voice sounded slurred and he took a gulp of wine, like he was trying to wash away a dry mouth.

"What are your favorites?" she asked.

"Well, I always liked steak and loaded baked potatoes."

"I like those, too," she allowed.

Grant leaned back in his chair, looking like he wished he hadn't eaten the excellent lunch he'd prepared. "I'm not feeling so good," he said in a voice he couldn't quite hold steady.

Jenny stared at him in concern. "Maybe you should go up and lie down," she said. Now that her plan was working, she wondered if sending him upstairs was really a good idea. What if he tripped on the stairs and fell?

Guilt grabbed her by the throat when he pressed the heel of his hand against one eye.

Pushing himself back from the table, he stood on shaky legs and tottered to the couch where he sat down heavily, then kicked off his shoes and swung his legs onto the cushions. "Need to take a little nap," he said in a barely audible voice as he pulled one of the side pillows under his head.

"Yes." Watching what she'd done to him made her physically ill, and she was glad she hadn't eaten much of the food. She'd crushed up two sleeping pills. Had she given him too much?

She crossed the room and knelt on the floor beside him. "Grant?"

He didn't answer, and she pressed her hand against his chest to make sure his heart was beating. To her relief, it felt strong and regular. Her hand moved to his pocket. Reaching inside, she found his keys and his wallet.

"Sorry," she whispered as she riffled through the wallet and took out about two hundred dollars before standing and backing away.

"I'm so sorry," she said again, staring at Grant's slack face. "Here I am stealing more money." She gulped. "But that's not the worst part. Grant, I love you. That's why I have to leave. If you knew who I really was, you'd hate me." She dragged in a breath and let it out. "I don't hold it against you, but I know you lied to me. I'm almost certain Carlos Mardano got away. He's a dangerous man, more dangerous than you can imagine. And he works for someone even more despicable. I've been running from that man, but now I know I have to do something about him—or die trying," she added in a whisper.

He didn't respond, and she crossed to him again. Kneeling down, she pressed her lips softly to his cheek. "Don't hate me."

While she could still make herself do it, she turned and ran toward the front door. Stopping at the nearby cabinet, she opened drawers and found the weapons he'd told her about. She took a Glock, checked the action, then loaded a magazine and shoved it into place. After taking an extra box of ammunition, she stepped out the door and closed it quietly behind her.

Outside, she headed for the car, climbed in and started the engine. With a feeling of unreality, she pointed the vehicle toward the gate where they'd entered.

Grant lay slack on the couch, like the victim of a drug overdose who would never wake again. But his muscles tensed, and as soon as he heard the car start outside, his eyes blinked open.

It had taken every ounce of control he possessed not to react to the things she was telling him. Now he was free to act.

He wanted to scream in frustration. Instead he pushed himself up and took a deep breath. He'd been pretty sure that Jenny was going to pull something. He stopped himself from using the word "stupid" and substituted "desperate."

Before they'd come here, the staff had brainstormed various possibilities, and Grant had been the one to suggest putting a bottle of fake sleeping pills in her medicine cabinet. Sugar pills actually, so he would be able to detect them. He'd hoped she wasn't going to use them. But as soon as she'd started asking for wine with lunch, he'd been suspicious. And the oversweet taste of what was in his glass clued him to what she had planned.

To keep her from figuring out that he was on to her, he'd gotten into a big tutorial about how to make mac and cheese.

It had worked, even as he'd felt like he was having a conversation in a madhouse.

That had been weird enough. Then he'd watched her watching him as he went into his drugged wine act. After that, she'd done what he expected—with one big exception.

She hadn't thought he could even hear her, but she'd said she loved him.

His heart squeezed. "Damn you, Jenny," he growled. "You picked a hell of a time to tell me that. And a hell of a time to run out on me. I can't help you unless you let me."

The next part was worse. Through slitted eyes, he'd watched her take a gun and ammo from the cabinet near the door. And from what she'd said, he was pretty sure her plan was to eliminate the threat to Decorah Security from Carlos and his boss, probably the guy named Rambo.

This time she wasn't simply running away. Terror leaped inside his chest. She was going to put herself in danger—even if it meant she wasn't going to survive.

While all that was running through his mind, he was heading for the back of the house, to the garage where another car was parked. Climbing in, he activated the surveillance system that would focus on the car Jenny had taken. It was a camera mounted on the front of the vehicle that showed where she was going. He had another weapon at his disposal. In addition to the camera, there was a GPS tracker on the car so that he would know her exact location.

But he was going to have to give her a head start so that she wouldn't know he was on her trail.

He could have counted to three hundred in his mind while he gave Jenny some breathing room. Instead he reached out to his brother.

Mack, are you there, Mack?

His heart pounded while he waited for his brother to respond. Finally he heard the familiar voice in his head. *What do you need, Grant?*

Jenny's skipped out of the safe house like we thought she would, and she's on her way to the gate. This time I think she's not just running away. I think she's going to kill the guy who kidnapped her.

Jesus!

Yeah. But this is our chance to find out where she came from. I'm going to follow her. And I have some information. The thug who got away is Carlos Mardano. Get Teddy to look him up.

Okay. But, uh, you're not stupid enough to try and handle this by yourself.

Grant answered with a grim laugh. *No. There's a GPS tracker in the extra car, too. Get a team together and follow me.*

Will do.

Gotta go. I'll talk to you when I know something.

The driveway was long, but he'd been watching Jenny as she headed for what she thought was freedom. She had pulled up at the gate.

Using the remote camera, he watched her press the button that would open the barrier from the inside. Then she was off the safe house property and heading for the two-lane road that led to the property.

He had to let her reach it before he gave chase. If she knew he was coming after her, that would screw up his plan.

Before she got more than a fifty yards down the driveway, a car shot out of the woods, blocking her path, and she slammed to a stop to avoid crashing into it.

CHAPTER TWENTY

"Jesus."

Mack must have still been lurking around because he heard the exclamation.

What?

A car pulled out in front of her. Gotta go.

With the camera in Jenny's car, he could see men closing in on either side of her vehicle. She looked momentarily dazed, then pulled out the weapon she'd taken from the safe house.

But both doors of the vehicle were yanked open simultaneously. And the man she had called Carlos Mardano grabbed her and slapped something over her face.

Grant gripped the weapon he'd brought with him, but he couldn't rush in and shoot, not when Jenny was in his line of fire.

Cursing, he could only watch the drama unfold. When she had gone slack, the two men conferred. A minute later, the man Grant didn't recognize climbed back into the car that had blocked her path. Carlos still held Jenny. He folded her into the car she'd been driving, and both vehicles roared away.

"Christ."

His brother was still there. *What happened?*

The one named Carlos took her away in the car she stole. The other guy is in the second vehicle. But it means we can track her.

Right.

Grant swallowed hard. *I have to give them a head start. Then I can follow.*

And we'll be right after you.

Unable to keep talking with anyone, even his twin, Grant signed off and pounded on the steering wheel. Everything had happened so fast that he'd barely had time to make decisions.

Now he struggled to fill in the whole picture. Somehow, the Carlos guy hadn't been fooled by the ambulance ploy. He'd known it wasn't Jenny being taken away. Or maybe he hadn't been sure, and he'd sent the other thug to report. Which meant they'd been somewhere lurking near the Decorah offices. But how come Grant hadn't spotted a tail?

As he went back over the events of the day before, he remembered the traffic tie-up. Son of a bitch. What if the guy had caused the accident, then waited for Grant to catch up. And the two men had used a tag team approach to follow?

"Shit!"

He'd been too confident.

Not just you, Mack commented.

Get the hell out of my head.

He felt his brother withdraw. Well not entirely. He was still lurking around while he was organizing a team to follow Grant.

He wanted to rush after Jenny, but that would probably only get him captured. What he had to do now was keep calm and bide his time.

As he tried to bring his blood pressure under control, an idea flitted into his head. He'd been in telepathic communication with Jenny while she'd been sleeping. And the Carlos guy had knocked her out with something. Did that give Grant a chance to contact her now?

Jenny, he tried, *Jenny, can you hear me?*

When he got no answer, he wanted to shout in frustration, but he forced himself to stay calm. He tried several more times, but nothing happened.

"Shit," he muttered again.

That hadn't worked, but at least he finally thought it was safe to follow her. Starting the engine, he headed for the gate, keeping one eye on the tracking device.

The car with Jenny was heading north. And probably the other one, too. He'd have to make sure neither guy spotted him.

As he reached the gate, his phone buzzed, and he looked at the caller ID. It was Teddy from the Decorah IT department.

"What have you got for me?" he demanded as he pushed the release that opened the barrier. While Teddy kept talking, Grant drove through and closed the gate behind him.

"Glad she coughed up the Carlos Mardano name. He has a criminal record. Mob stuff. Illegal gambling. Robbing trucks carrying premium goods. And he's gotten caught several times beating the crap out of guys from rival organizations."

"Shit. And he's got Jenny."

"He's likely taking her to the estate of Malcolm Oakland."

"That's Rambo? How do you know?"

"Well, I don't know for sure, but Carlos works for the guy. He's the boss of his organization."

"Which does what?"

"Same stuff Carlos is into. Plus drugs, prostitution."

"Christ. Sounds like a nice guy."

Teddy made a commiserative sound.

Grant was still trying to get a handle on Oakland. "And he's not young?"

"He's in his sixties, but he keeps himself in good shape."

"You got a picture."

"Yeah. Moments later, a photo appeared on Grant's phone screen. It was of a trim man with hair obviously dyed dark, a candid shot, probably taken with a telephoto lens.

Grant studied the picture, which had been taken at a garden party or some other outdoor event.

"Is he the one who kidnapped her?" Grant asked, thinking she had told him it was a younger man who had a child in elementary school. Of course a guy in his sixties could have a young child, too. But had she told the story but changed some of the details about the man?

"Don't know," Teddy answered.

"Okay, but you have the address of the estate? In case somehow I lose her on the GPS tracker."

"Yes. It's in a posh section of Morristown." Teddy gave him the address. "We can send a drone over to get some pictures."

"Right. Great idea."

He had pulled over to talk to Teddy. When they ended the conversation he took off again, glad that he had a destination. But that didn't help with his fear for Jenny. He'd seen firsthand what kind of guy Carlos was. But hopefully, in this case, he was just the messenger, charged with delivering a captive to Malcolm Oakland—presumably the Rambo guy. And then what? As far as Grant knew now, Jenny had run away from Oakland. And he'd gone to a lot of trouble to have her brought back. So he could keep her for himself? Or to punish her?

Grant shuddered. He was pretty sure Jenny had planned to show up unexpectedly and kill Oakland. Which made her desperate to sever the relationship. What did that say about the man? And Grant had another question. Why would Oakland trust her to get near him?

Too many unknowns swirled in Grant's head. But all he could do was keep driving, praying that nothing bad was going to happen to Jenny before he could get her out of there.

* * *

About a half hour out from the estate, Grant's cell phone buzzed again.

"We're here," Brand Marshall said.

"Huh?"

"Well, in the vicinity. About three miles down the road, so the guy won't know we're focused on him."

"How did you beat me?"

"We flew. Not practical for invading, but good for speed."

"Yeah."

Brand told him where they were, and he headed for the meeting spot. It seemed to be in a residential neighborhood, and he was shocked to see it was a long, low red-brick ranch house with a large wooded lot in an upscale community where all the homes looked custom built.

When he climbed out of the car, he found Brand, Cole, Mack, Ben Walker, and Frank waiting for him in the driveway, which led to a three-car garage. They had driven from the local airport in two SUV's.

"What are you doing here? Did you break into the house?" he asked.

Frank answered. "Nothing so dramatic. I talked to a real estate agent before I left Maryland and was able to arrange a short-term rental. I figure we could use a base of operations. Come on in."

The interior was furnished in a traditional style, hardwood floors, Oriental rugs, comfortable chairs and sofas, and a large flat-screen TV in the family room. Grant dropped gratefully onto one of the couches facing the television. It was tempting to throw his head back and close his eyes for a few moments. Instead he asked the assembled group,

"You got any more information?"

Cole answered. "We've got video from the drone."

"Okay. That's good. Let's see it."

"You should probably give yourself a little breathing room," Mack said.

Grant glared at him. "I'll take some breathing room when Jenny is safe."

Frank nodded. "We started with a flyover of the estate. But then we got lucky and spotted a car arriving. It turned out that was the guy bringing Jenny."

"Is she okay?" Grant almost shouted.

"She was standing on her own two feet when she got out of the car. They hustled her into the house."

"Let me see."

Mack gaze him a sympathetic look. Ben put a CD into a player attached to the TV and turned both on. Grant gripped the edge of his chair as he watched the drone circle around a huge house, wide green lawns, a pool and tennis courts, all surrounded by a high iron fence. Then a car entered the compound. A man he recognized from the picture of Malcolm Oakland came out of the house. Carlos pulled Jenny from the car. Her hands were cuffed, and her head was downcast.

Oakland must have said something because her gaze jerked up, and she and Oakland stood facing each other. He seemed to be talking, his expression angry. Then he spoke to Carlos, and the underling marched Jenny through the front door and out of view. After that, the picture froze.

Grant closed his eyes for a moment. "At least I know she's alive." Then he turned to Frank. "How long ago was that?"

"Forty minutes," the Decorah chief answered as he pulled a chair closer to Grant.

"And what the hell does he want with her?"

"Sorry. We don't know," Ben answered.

In a hostile kidnap situation like this, Grant knew that forty minutes could be a lifetime. He also knew that rushing in without a plan could get Jenny killed.

CHAPTER TWENTY-ONE

Grant glanced at the TV. The shot of Oakland standing alone in front of the house was still frozen on the screen. A bolt of anger shot through Grant, and it was all he could do to keep himself from throwing something at the hateful image. The man looked arrogant, sure of his power, and sure that the thugs who worked for him would carry out his orders without question.

"We'll get her back," Frank said, his voice deep and reassuring.

"How?"

"Maybe she can help."

Grant dragged in a breath and let it out. "How?"

"In your report, you said you were able to communicate with Jenny—mind to mind."

"Yesterday," he spat out. "Today it didn't work."

"What did you do yesterday?"

"I ... I," he stopped and looked around the room, aware that everybody was watching the exchange. Although he had wanted to keep some information private, he knew that if he was going to help Jenny, he had to give his friends the facts they needed. But maybe there was a way to keep the X-rated part private.

He dragged in a breath and let it out before saying, "When we drove over to the safe house from Decorah headquarters, we weren't saying much to each other. She went up to bed, and I stayed downstairs to work. When she went to sleep, she was dreaming about a place that looked like the VR. Somehow she pulled me in." He ran a hand through his hair. "It wasn't really the VR. It was her ... recreation of it because I think she felt safe in that environment. We were ... together there," he said, not catching anyone's gaze and deliberately leaving out key details. "But when I tried to reach out to her on the way up here, I couldn't make any progress."

"You're sure that wasn't just your dream?" Frank asked.

"No. When we woke up, she came downstairs, and we talked about it. We were together in the dream. But I couldn't do it today."

"Well, the conditions certainly weren't ideal, since you had to be focused on driving. But now that you can relax here, I want you to try that again," Frank said gently.

"I ..."

"I mean lie down. Close your eyes. Go into a simulation of the VR and see if you can get her to meet you there."

Grant dragged in another breath and let it out. "I guess it's worth a shot." He looked around the room. "And while I'm trying to do that—you'll be working on a plan to get her out of Oakland's clutches?"

"Yes," Frank said.

Grant was torn. He wanted to be in on the strategy session, but at the same time he knew Frank had a point. He had a chance to do something nobody else could, something that might make a crucial difference in getting Jenny out of there alive.

"Okay."

"Go into one of the bedrooms. See what you can do," Frank said, reinforcing the words with an encouraging hand on Grant's shoulder.

163

He felt like a man who had fallen off the side of a cliff and was grasping at branches and clumps of vegetation, trying to stop his downward plummet. But he had learned to trust Frank's judgment. And just maybe he could do this—if he was desperate enough.

Grant left the rest of the Decorah agents in the media room and walked down a hallway, looking into the bedrooms. There were four, each with its own bath. He chose the master, which had a king-size bed and drapes he could pull across the windows to shut out the light. After darkening the room, he folded back the spread, arranged a couple of pillows to cradle his head and kicked off his shoes. Lying down, he let himself sink into comfortable mattress. He had hardly gotten any sleep the night before. Then he'd driven up here in a reckless dash. Now that he was lying down, he had to fight to keep from drifting off. But he gathered his focus and started picturing the VR. He went in through the room Lily had set up as a transition. From there he walked into the lobby, greeted the woman behind the desk the way he had on his last visit, and hurried out the back of the building and down to the pool area. There he stepped into the cabana where he and Jenny had made love. Only this was the version she had conjured up—a bedroom that was much more opulent than the original.

He felt his chest tighten as he looked around the beautifully appointed space. He had held Jenny in his arms here last night. And he would again, he vowed, as he climbed into the bed.

It had been easy to take himself to this place. Now he faced the hard part. He thought about how Jenny had called him to this bedroom. Not by using words. One moment he had been in the great room of the safe house. In the next, he had been holding her in his arms—here.

"Jenny," he murmured as he imagined her with him, lying on this bed, reaching out to him.

When long moments passed and nothing changed, he clamped his teeth together to keep from screaming in frustration.

With a sense of defeat, he pushed himself up and opened his eyes. The view was a sudden shock. He had been in the fancy bed chamber Jenny had designed for the two of them. Now he was back in the house where the Decorah agents were camped out. And they were all down the hall, hoping he could connect with Jenny. Too bad it hadn't worked.

With a groan, he swung his legs off the bed, stood up and crossed to the bathroom, where he turned on the water in the sink and splashed some onto his face before drying off. When he raised his eyes and looked in the mirror, he saw a man with bloodshot eyes and the dark shadow of a beard.

Maybe he was too tired. Maybe there was no way to make this work. But he wasn't going to give up until he had exhausted every avenue.

Returning to the bed, he eased down again and lay for a few moments with his eyes closed, imagining himself back in the VR bedroom.

"Jenny, I want to be with you again. I know you left the safe house because you thought you had to. Maybe you thought I was better off without you. But it's not true. I love you. I want to be with you." He stopped, letting that reality sink in before continuing. "You're in danger now. I can help you, but you have to come back to me. In your mind. The way we did it last night," he whispered.

As he spoke, he tried to make his imagination more vivid. Breathing deeply, he pictured Jenny lying beside him on the bed.

Could he smell her unique scent? Could he hear her take a ragged breath?

When he felt the mattress shift, his heart leaped. Still afraid to open his eyes, he slowly reached out—and felt her warm body. Gently he cupped his hand over her shoulder, feeling the warmth of her skin and the strong muscles below.

With a sigh, he ran his fingertips down her arm, brushed against her ribs, her hip.

He was still afraid to open his eyes and find he was making it all up. Yet her body felt so real. And when he wrapped his arms around her, she molded herself against him.

"Jenny, thank God."

"Grant?"

When she spoke his name, he still couldn't be sure if he was creating the whole experience, or if he had really brought her here.

"Grant?" she said again.

His lids snapped open and he found himself staring into her face. She was wearing an almost transparent gown of some gauzy material.

Like him, she looked as though she couldn't quite believe that they were in the fantasy room again.

"Is it really you?" she asked. "I'm not just imagining this?"

"No. It's really me"

"Where are we?" she whispered.

"In the same room that you made last night."

"How?"

"I think because we both wanted it so much." He swallowed hard. "Jenny, we belong together."

"Are you sure?"

He answered her question with one of his own. "Why did you leave?"

"I knew I was risking your life by staying."

He tried to think what to say next. He wanted to tell her that she'd taken a terrible chance by leaving the safe house, but he saw no point in accusations

"Are you all right?" he asked.

Her voice was hesitant. "I don't know."

"Is Malcolm Oakland going to hurt you?"

She caught her breath. "You know his name?"

"Yes."

"How?"

"You told me the name of the guy who came after you— Carlos Mardano. He works for Oakland."

She answered with a small nod. Then her eyes widened. "You heard that?"

"Yes."

"How?"

He swallowed hard. "I was afraid you were going to try and run away again, and I thought about how you might do it. The sleeping pills in your bathroom were fakes."

"Oh," she said in a small voice.

"I'm sorry. I had to keep you safe."

"By lying to me?" Her image shimmered, and he was afraid she was going to disappear.

Gripping her shoulders, he said, "I think we each did things we weren't proud of because we were each trying to protect the other." Quickly he continued. "You don't have time to be angry with me now. Do it later after we get you out of there."

His heart pounded as she considered that, then gave a little nod. "Okay."

He let out the breath he'd been holding. "Who is Oakland? And why does he want to hurt you?"

"Because I disobeyed him, and anyone who does that must be punished."

"And what is he to you?"

She made a strangled sound but kept her gaze steady. "He's my father."

Grant couldn't hold back a sharp exclamation. "Did I hear that right? Your father? This is all about your father?"

"Yes."

"I've heard so many stories from you; why should I believe this one?"

Her face contorted. "It's the one that I couldn't force myself to say, so I made stuff up."

Still trying to come to terms with this new reality, he said, "You don't have the same last name."

"I told you my parents were dead. Really, my mom managed to get away one night—with the help of a guard she seduced, I think. Or maybe they were in love. I have her last name because she and my father never married. And if you know who he is, you must know he's a big New Jersey crime boss."

Grant nodded.

"She hooked up with him, then realized she'd made a big mistake." She sighed. "He can be charming when he wants to be. But after she was living at the estate, she discovered what he was really like. He runs the place with an iron hand. And his sister, my Aunt Sophie, helps." she paused. "Or she did. I think he sent Auntie away after I ran. Or maybe he killed her because she didn't keep a good enough eye on me."

He shuddered. "Your father would kill his sister?"

"He'd kill anyone."

Grant tried to absorb her words before asking. "Your mom didn't take you with her when she left?"

Jenny's expression grew sad. "I think she loved me—sort of. But when it came to her getting away, she knew she had a better chance without me, because Dad had decided he wanted to hang on to me. When I was a little girl, he didn't give a fig about me. But later I became important to him. Not because he loved me, but because he saw me as a valuable commodity. He wanted to cement his relationship with another mob because his guys and their guys were killing each other. And he figured the best way to do it was to marry his daughter to the son of the rival boss."

"So that stuff about your being a teacher and meeting the father of one of your students was..."

"A lie," she finished for him. "I couldn't bear to tell you the truth—that he arranged for me to meet Gabe at a party. He was interested in me. I thought he was a legitimate businessman. I did like him. He seemed nice. And I guess my father figured that after we were together and he got me pregnant, I'd stick with him."

She began speaking faster, as though she wanted to get the explanation over with. "You asked if he raped me. Not in the sense of forcing me. I thought he was my chance to escape from the life of a gangster's daughter. I let him seduce me, and then I found out that he was the son of Winston Thompson, and father and son were into the same intimidation and killing and drug dealing as my dad. When I realized I'd jumped from the frying pan into the fire, I couldn't stand that I'd fallen into the trap Gabe and my father set. I tried to get away. But I didn't make it very far, and you know the rest," she said in a defeated voice. "And now you know for sure what kind of woman you've gotten mixed up with."

"Christ, Jenny, none of that is your fault."

"I was so naive."

When she tried to slide away from him, he pulled her close. Folding her in his arms, he rocked her gently on the bed.

She was rigid in his embrace for a few moments. Then she relaxed against him.

"You're a good man, Grant Bradley," she whispered.

"And you're a good woman."

"No."

"Don't beat yourself up for what your father's done."

"I ..."

"Let's focus on getting you out of there. But first," he covered her lips with his for a long, hot kiss.

When they broke apart, she hitched a breath.

"That's a down payment on what I have planned for you," he said. "But we have to spring you. I'm near your father's estate with a bunch of Decorah agents."

"And he could kill me—and then all of you."

"Your father would kill you?" he asked, hearing the incredulity in his own voice.

"When I said he could get rid of anyone, I meant it. You don't know what he does to people who cross him. If Gabe Thompson doesn't want me now, I've ruined Dad's plans."

"Jesus." The idea of Oakland killing his own daughter—Jenny to be exact—was sickening. But Grant wouldn't let it happen. "You're going to help us pull it off. "

His mind scrambled for order. He had a lot to do, and they'd better deal with the most urgent business first.

"We took a video of the estate from a drone. It's as luxurious as the Mirador hotel."

"Uh huh. The Mirador was like the luxury I was used to. But I was punished if I was 'bad.'"

He wanted to know about that, but what he had to do now was focus on the current situation.

Where are you in the house?"

"In my bedroom."

"Which is where?"

"As you're facing the mansion, it's in the wing on the left."

"Okay."

He kept asking questions in rapid succession.

"Are there a lot of bedrooms over there?"

"Five. Mine is at the end of the hall."

"Anything else that would help us find you quickly?"

"There's a bed of expensive hybrid rosebushes outside my window."

"Good. And how many men can we expect to find in the house?"

"My father and probably four security guys."

"Armed with?"

"Automatic handguns. And automatic rifles if they need them."

"Good to know." He swallowed hard. "When Carlos brought you in, you were in handcuffs."

"How do you know that?"

170

"From the drone. It happened to be there when you arrived."

"Are you still handcuffed?"

"Yes."

"And you're wearing that gown?"

"Yes. I guess he figured I wasn't going escape half naked with my hands cuffed."

Grant winced. "We should get you out of those cuffs."

"How?"

"I'll show you. You're cuffed with your hands in front of you, right?"

"Yes."

"Okay, that makes it easier because you can see what you're doing." He shifted so he could reach the drawer of the small table beside the bed. From inside, he pulled out a pair of handcuffs and a large paper clip.

Jenny started at the objects. "Where did those come from?"

He laughed. "I guess I put them there. I mean, I made this place. Well, it's a copy of the room you created last night. But this one's mine, and I can bring in anything I want."

She nodded.

He held up the police-issue cuffs. "Basic handcuffs work by moving a rounded ridged bar into a ratchet with ridges which keep the lock from opening. To unlock the handcuffs, you use a key to push the ridges inside so the bar can slide back.

"But we can use a paper clip, bobby pin or something similar instead of a key."

He opened up one end of the paper clip, inserted it in the lock, and bent it at a right angle to make an L.

"Now we can stick the end part of the L inside the lock and turn it like a key to push down the inside ridges."

He locked the cuffs and demonstrated what he'd just told her. The cuffs snapped open. Locking them again, he handed them to her along with the paper clip.

"Try it."

She inserted the end in the keyhole and moved it around a bit, feeling for the ridges. When the lock snapped open, she grinned at him in triumph.

"Try it again."

She practiced several more times.

"Do you have a paper clip in your room?"

"On my old school papers."

All at once, he could see a change in her expression.

"What?"

"He's coming. I can't be here."

"Wait."

The word was barely out of his mouth, when she disappeared from beside him. One moment she was on the bed and in the next she was simply gone.

CHAPTER TWENTY-TWO

Jenny swung around on the bed in her room so that she was facing the door. When he father stepped inside, she forced herself not to shrink away.

"Are you satisfied, bitch?" he asked.

"About what?" she replied, struggling to keep her voice steady.

"All you had to do was marry Gabe Thompson. You liked him. He was fine in bed. But no. You decided you were too good for him."

"Not too good," she whispered.

"Oh yeah. And how would you put it?"

She was sorry she had protested. Better to let him rant and get some of the anger out of his system, because anything she said was going to make him angrier.

"Answer me," he spat out.

"It wasn't the kind of marriage I wanted."

"Oh, that's just fine." He glared at her. "It wasn't your decision to make."

When she remained silent, he shouted, "Say something."

"I'm sorry," she managed. She wasn't sorry for what she had done. She was sorry that he'd found her and hauled her back—and that he knew she'd been with Decorah Security.

"I'm going to make sure you're damn sorry," he said. "I'm sure Gabe doesn't trust you enough to have you for a wife. But I can give you to him to do whatever he wants. And as far as I'm concerned, that can be *anything*."

She sucked in a sharp breath.

"And I'm going to find that bastard who was helping you out and cut his balls off before I carve up the rest of him."

She couldn't hold back a gasp—which drew a look of satisfaction from her father.

When he turned and stomped out of the room, she clamped her hands into fists. She had left the Decorah safe house with a gun, thinking she was going to shoot this man. Then she'd thought that maybe if she held him at gunpoint, she could reason with him.

For years she had sensed that he was a bad person without knowing precisely why. Now she knew he was beyond bad. He was almost the definition of evil. And she knew for sure that there was only one way to end his vicious behavior.

Grant reached out to where Jenny had been lying. The sheets felt warm, but she was no longer there. He moved over and buried his face in the bedding. He longed to call her back, but he knew that was the wrong thing to do. She needed to speak to her father, and it would be dangerous to have her missing in action.

With a sigh, he heaved himself off the bed, exited the room, and walked down the hall to the living area.

As he blocked the light from the hallway, everybody looked up expectantly.

"It worked," Frank said.

"How do you know?"

"From your face."

Grant nodded. "Yes, I pulled her into the ..." He rocked his hand back and forth, "The fake VR with me. We talked, but she had to go back—because the guy who had her snatched up was coming back."

"So who kidnapped her?" Cole asked.

He swallowed before answering. "It's complicated. Her father gave her to a guy who turned out to be a thug. She ran away, and her dad was determined to bring her back—and make her sorry she ran."

The men stared at him, some looking like they didn't believe it was true.

"This is all about her father?" Cole said. "You mean she's not really in danger?"

"She's in danger, all right. Imminent danger. He sees her as a slave who disobeyed her master. She's wearing a flimsy gown, handcuffed, and locked in her room. I showed her how to unlock the cuffs." Grant filled them in on what Jenny had told him about her relationship with Oakland and his sister and how her mother had managed to escape.

"Jesus," Ben said.

"Oakland's got at least four men," Grant added. "Well armed. Just rushing in there could get one of you killed."

"We were talking about a diversion, to pull the guards away from the house."

"Like what?"

We're bringing in a larger drone with a payload. We'll drop a bomb in the garden area in back of the swimming pool. Some of the guards will rush over. Some will stay. But we'll take them by surprise—with a couple of wolves."

"Yeah, good thinking, but I want to try something that will help—if I can do it."

When Frank raised an inquiring eyebrow, he went on, "I brought Jenny into the VR with me. If I can reverse it—go to where she is—then I can contact Mack and tell you exactly what's going on in the house."

"You think you can do it?" Frank asked.

"I don't know, but give me a chance to try."

Frank pinned him with a sharp look. "Okay, but you're the one who thinks we don't have much time."

"Right." Grant turned and hurried back to the bedroom. Lying down on the bed again, he reached for the place where Jenny had been lying. The sheet was barely warm now, but he felt the ghost of her presence there.

Closing his eyes, he focused on the woman he loved. The way she looked. The way she tasted. The way she felt in his arms. And the way she had tried to run away because she thought she had put Decorah Security in jeopardy simply by being alive.

That thought made his chest squeeze.

"Jenny," he whispered. "Don't you know how much I want to be with you?"

In his mind he kept reaching out toward her, kept speaking to her. For long minutes nothing happened, and he thought he'd have to go back to the other agents in defeat. Then he heard her voice in his head. It was low and far away, but he heard her.

Grant? Is that you?

Yes.

Where are you?

Keep talking to me. Try to pull me closer to you.

I don't know how.

Neither of us knows how. Just reach out like you want to hold me in your arms.

He wasn't sure how to reach her. All he could do was follow the advice he'd given Jenny. Only he had a small advantage because he had spent years communicating mind to mind with his brother. Still, it wasn't easy. When her voice grew louder, his pulse beat faster.

That's it. I think it's working. Keep pulling me in—like you did last night in the place like the VR. Like I pulled you in today.

He kept speaking to her, so she could use his voice as a guidepost. He seemed to be in some place with no light and no sound except her voice. Then he saw a spot of brightness, like a door had opened at the end of a tunnel. He rushed forward, and all at once he was standing in a bedroom.

"Jenny, thank God," he breathed as he reached for her.

She looked shocked to see that he was there, but she came into his arms, clinging to him.

He wanted to keep holding her, but they had work to do.

When he eased away, he looked around the room. It was a frilly little girl's room, with white French furniture and a bedspread and curtains in shades of pink.

"Jesus. This looks like a room for a ten year old."

"It was. My mom decorated it for me when I was eight. She left when I was ten, and my father never changed it."

"How did you keep from going crazy?"

She answered with a small laugh. "I had a lot of interests. I read. I made pottery... I learned how to make window panels out of stained glass. I guess I have a lot of artistic talents."

He looked at her and saw that she'd taken off the handcuffs and had pulled open several drawers in a cabinet under the window.

"What are you doing?"

"Looking for a weapon." She gulped. "He said he was going to give me to Gabe Thompson to do anything he wanted with me, and he said he was going to ... cut you to pieces. I have to stop him. And I think I can do it, because he assumes I'm so cowed that I won't do anything to fight him."

"He doesn't know you're not the scared woman who first came to the VR."

"Not hardly."

He stepped to the cabinet and put his hand on one of the open drawers. He could barely feel it. And when he whacked his palm against the wood, it seemed to go partly through.

He looked from his hand to the drawer. "I can't really touch anything here—except you."

"I see. It's weird."

"Let me tell Mack the situation. Then we'll figure out what to do."

He closed his eyes, reaching out to his brother who was apparently standing by, waiting for the contact.

Grant?

Yeah. I'm in her bedroom. Sort of. I can touch her, but I can't touch anything else.

Okay, what if we have the drone drop its payload in twenty minutes?

Fine.

He broke off the communication and looked back at Jenny. "They're using a drone to drop a bomb on the property in twenty minutes. We need to get out of this room." He sighed. "Well, you need to get out. Unfortunately, I'm not really here. I mean, I can't do anything physical—like, for example, break the door down. And, uh, maybe you want to put on some clothes."

Grant felt a sudden wave of dizziness. For a moment the scene around him shimmered, and he thought he was going to lose the connection with Jenny's surroundings. Desperately, he clung to the scene and finally, he was able to make it stabilize.

"What happened?" Jenny gasped out.

"I thought I was being pulled out of here."

"Why?"

"I don't know. But it's okay now."

"Good."

She crossed to a dresser, and took out underwear and a tee shirt and jeans. Then she took off the gown and dressed.

As she pulled on her shoes, she said, "I learned how to escape from this room a long time ago. I used to walk around the house and go outside in the middle of the night. From the table beside the bed, she picked up the paper clip she'd used to open the handcuffs and started toward the door. Before she reached it the knob turned.

Jenny froze.

178

Grant's impulse was to put himself between her and the door. But what good would that do? He had no physical presence here.

Jenny backed away toward one of the open drawers and reached inside. He saw her take out some kind of small craft knife and hold it down beside her leg.

The door opened and a man stepped into the room. He had dyed black hair and a lined face, but his body was fit and trim. It was the man in the photograph, the man who had met her when Carlos brought her in. As her father stared at Jenny his expression darkened.

From where he stood in the corner, Grant reached out to his brother.

Mack, if you can drop the bomb now, do it. If you can hear me, drop the bomb now.

Without waiting for a reply, he switched his attention back to the bedroom.

"What the hell? How did you get out of those handcuffs?" Oakland demanded.

"Magic."

"Don't get smart with me, young lady. I didn't give you permission to get dressed."

Grant stepped into the conversation. "Yes, magic," he confirmed, as he lunged toward the angry man, waving his arms and making bellowing sounds. His fist would have connected with the man's chin if he'd really been in the room. Instead, it kind of glanced off.

Dad stopped in his tracks, his hand fingering his chin. "What the hell is that?"

"It's me, you son of a bitch," Grant shouted. He didn't know what Oakland was seeing, hearing and feeling from him, but it was obviously *something*.

Still Grant was only a momentary distraction. After the ghostly encounter, Oakland started forward again, his hands raised as though he intended to choke the life out of Jenny. As her father advanced on her, she brought the hand with the knife up, slashing through his white dress shirt and into his arm.

"You bitch." He jumped away and pulled a gun, pointing it at her chest outside.

CHAPTER TWENTY-THREE

Grant watched in horror, knowing there was no way for him to stop the man from shooting his daughter.

Still, he tried. "Over here," he shouted, lunging forward again.

Oakland's attention wavered toward him, and he planted himself in the guy's face. The man blinked "What the hell is that?"

"Like I said, magic," Jenny answered, her voice surprisingly even.

"Yeah, well I'll take care of that for you."

Grant knew he was about to shoot, but before he could pull the trigger, an explosion outside shook the house.

The people in the room, wavered on their feet as a shock wave ballooned from the site of the impact. Oakland tumbled backwards. Grant caught Jenny before she could go down. With his help, she righted herself quickly, dashed toward her father, snatched the gun from his hand, and darted back.

Now she was the one holding the weapon on him.

"Put that down," he bellowed.

"Not a chance. Get up. We're going outside."

"The hell we are. You don't have the guts to shoot me."

"Don't bet on it."

181

She could have killed him, but when he started toward her with his face grim and his hands raised, she fired, striking him in the arm she had already cut. He bellowed in pain and rage.

"Let's go. And no more funny stuff," she said again. "Or next time I'm going to aim for center mass."

Grimacing in pain, Oakland steadied himself against the back of a chair.

"Where should we go?" Jenny asked Grant.

"What do you mean, where should we go?" the mobster asked. "Who the hell are you talking to?"

"My fairy godfather."

"The front door," Grant answered.

Oakland blinked. "What was that?"

"More magic."

"Be careful when we get outside this room," Grant warned. "The plan was to get most of the guards outside. But some could still be in here with the boss.

To prove it, one of them came charging down the hall, a gun in his hand.

Behind him was one of the Marshalls in wolf form. The animal leaped on the thug, bringing him down. Behind the wolf was Ben Walker, automatic pistol in hand.

The wolf stepped back and Ben ordered, "Put the gun on the floor and stand up slowly."

The guy did as he was ordered.

Grant made a low sound. It had been a good idea to come here by using his mental connection with Jenny, but now he was out of the action.

No, his brother said inside his head. *We brought you along. You're in the SUV in the driveway.*

Thanks

"Be right back," he said to Jenny, thinking that when they'd moved him, he'd almost come back to his body. That was why the scene around him had wavered a little while ago.

It happened again now, only he was the one in control. And this time, when his eyes blinked open, he found himself sitting in the front passenger seat of an SUV.

He yanked the door open, then had to steady himself when he felt light-headed.

From across the lawn, he could see smoke rising in a black column. As he started toward the house, he saw a man running across the lawn. It was Carlos, the thug who had abducted Jenny. When the guy saw Grant, he started shooting.

Grant ducked behind the car, cursing. He'd come here unarmed.

No wait. That was wrong. When he felt for the gun in his shoulder holster, he found the Sig nestled inside.

He clicked off the safety and ducked around the hood of the car, returning fire. Carlos tried to dodge behind a tree, but Grant got him first, and he went down.

Looking around to make sure nobody else had drawn a bead on him, Grant made for the house. In the living room, he found Ben and the wolf standing guard over the security guy.

Which left Jenny and her father still in the hall.

Probably the Decorah men thought the emergency was over. Grant wasn't so sure. He arrived in time to see Oakland pull a small caliber pistol from a holster at his ankle and aim it at Jenny.

Only an expert marksman could take the shot. Neither Grant nor Jenny hesitated. They both fired at the same time, both of them hitting the mob boss, who went slack on the floor.

Grant rushed to Jenny and pulled her away, into another bedroom. Clasping her in his arms, he held on tight.

"Are you okay?" both of them asked at the same time.

"Yes," they both answered.

Then his lips came down on hers for a hot, savage kiss.

When they broke apart, they saw Frank Decorah standing in the doorway.

"Are we all secure?" Grant asked.

"Yes. But there's the question of what to do with the rest of Oakland's security guys."

"How many are left?" Jenny asked.

"Two."

"Put them in a plane and fly them to the Alaska. Let them off and turn them loose."

Frank laughed. "I like the way you think. That could actually work. At any rate, you've been through enough. Let us take care of the details."

"Thank you," she said, then added with a note of wonder in her voice, "I guess everything turned out okay."

"Yeah, well, sorry we had to make you think Carlos was dead after he broke into the patient facility. It's true now," Frank said.

She hung her head. "I should have trusted you. I was just too scared to take a chance."

"Everybody understands the position you were in." Frank looked toward the door. "I've got to supervise the ... clean up. You and Grant go enjoy your freedom."

"Amen," Grant agreed.

"Take one of the SUV's."

Jenny felt a sense of unreality as they climbed into the black vehicle.

"Is it really over?" she asked when Grant started the engine and pointed the car down the drive.

"Yeah. You're free."

"What about Gabe Thompson?"

"What's the point of his going after you now that your father's dead?"

"That makes sense," she answered, staring straight ahead through the windshield.

"But you're still worried about something," Grant said, his voice gentle.

"I lied to you about so much. Like—I was never a teacher. I was never anything but the Princess in the Tower."

"And now you have the freedom to do anything you want." She glanced at him, then away.

"And you have the money to do it."

"I don't want his money."

"I knew you'd say that. But think of it as victim's compensation. Like when someone is wrongfully imprisoned. That's worth something per year."

"I ..."

"You don't have to decide right now." As he pulled onto the highway, he asked, "Where do you want to go?"

"Somewhere we can be together—if you still want me."

"Of course I do." He made a low sound. "Too bad we can't go somewhere as nice as that room you imagined for us."

"Anywhere will do."

"Not quite." He pulled over to the side of the road and used the GPS to locate a nearby upscale hotel. Then he headed there.

A half hour later, he had checked them into an opulent room. It wasn't quite as grand as their fantasy room, but it would definitely do.

The moment the door closed behind them, he reached for her.

She came into his arms, clinging to him with an intensity that made his heart sing.

"Jenny, I need you."

"And I need you."

He was too keyed up to go slowly with her now. He kissed her with an intensity that stunned him, and her response stunned him even more. They tore at each other's clothing, intent on feeling naked skin pressed to naked skin.

They staggered across the room together, and he paused long enough to pull the covers out of the way.

When they fell onto the bed, she guided him inside her. They moved frantically together, each of them driving the other to climax. And as she shuddered in his arms, he followed her over the edge.

In the aftermath of the storm, they lay together panting.

He moved enough to pull up the covers, and they clung together in the wide bed.

She was the one who spoke first. "Oh, Grant, I should have trusted you," she repeated what she'd said to Frank.

"You weren't raised to trust. Your mother left you. Your father treated you like a bargaining chip. From what you say, your Aunt Sophie was like a prison guard."

"But then I ended up in the VR, and I realized what a caring group of people could be like." Her breath hitched. "But in a way that made it worse, because I knew my father could kill everybody there."

"You're safe now."

"That's still sinking in."

He raised up, looking down at her. "And you can do anything you want—be anything you want."

"I want to be with you. I've known that for a long time, but I was afraid I'd get you killed."

"You didn't."

She swallowed hard. "You said those sleeping pills were fake."

"Yeah."

"You were waiting for me to do something stupid."

"Not stupid. Desperate."

She knitted her fingers with his. "I won't ever lie to you again."

It was his turn to look contrite. "And I won't lie to you."

"I understand why you did."

"But now neither one of us has to pretend—about anything."

She nodded against his shoulder, and he felt her relax. He knew there were still things to work out. But he also knew that they had the time they needed.

"Will you teach me to cook?" she murmured. "Like you taught me to shoot."

"Sure. I mean a guy wants his wife to have some homemaker skills."

"Your wife?"

"Am I moving too fast?"

"No. I used to daydream about being married to you. But I couldn't believe it would ever happen."

"Believe it," he murmured, gathering her close and letting his happiness expand to envelop them both.

"I feel that," she whispered.

"My joy?"

"And mine. It's so good."

"Yes," he answered, knowing that what he had found with this woman could never be duplicated.

THE END

AFTERWORD

Thank you for purchasing FOUND MISSING, I hope you enjoyed reading it as much as I loved writing it.

If you enjoy my books, do me a huge favor. Please go back to www.amazon.com, and leave an honest review. Authors live and die by their reviews. The few extra seconds it takes are really appreciated. Thank you!

DECORAH SECURITY SERIES
(sexy paranormal romantic suspense)
BY REBECCA YORK

#1. ON EDGE (e-book novella and Decorah prequel).
#2. DARK MOON (e-book and trade paperback novel).
#3. CHAINED (e-book novella).
#4. AMBUSHED (e-book short story).
#5. DARK POWERS (e-book and trade paperback novel).
#6. HOT AND DANGEROUS (e-book short story).
#7. AT RISK (e-book and trade paperback novel).
#8. CHRISTMAS CAPTIVE (e-book novella).
#9. DESTINATION WEDDING (e-book novella).
#10. RX MISSING (e-book and trade paperback novel).
#11. HUNTING MOON (e-book and trade paperback novel).
#12. TERROR MANSION (e-book novella).
#13. OUTLAW JUSTICE (a novella).

DECORAH SECURITY COLLECTION (e-book including *Ambushed, Hot and Dangerous, Chained,* and *Dark Powers*).

OFF-WORLD SERIES
(sexy science-fiction romance)
BY REBECCA YORK

#1. HERO'S WELCOME (e-book romance short story).
#2. NIGHTFALL (e-book romance novella).
#3. CONQUEST (e-book romance short story).
#4. ASSIGNMENT DANGER (e-book romance novella).
#5. CHRISTMAS HOME (e-book romance short story).
#6. FIRELIGHT CONFESSION (e-book romance novella).

OFF WORLD COLLECTION (e-book including *Nightfall, Hero's Welcome,* and *Conquest*).

PRAISE FOR REBECCA YORK

Rebecca York delivers page-turning suspense.
—Nora Roberts

Rebecca York never fails to deliver. Her strong characterizations, imaginative plots and sensuous love scenes have made fans of thousands of romance, romantic suspense and thriller readers.
—Chassie West

Rebecca York will thrill you with romance, kill you with danger and chill you with the supernatural.
—Patricia Rosemoor

(Rebecca York) is a real luminary of contemporary series romance
—Michael Dirda, The Washington Post Book World

Rebecca York's writing is fast-paced, suspenseful, and loaded with tension.
—Jayne Ann Krentz

ABOUT REBECCA YORK

A New York Times and USA Today Best-Selling Author, Rebecca York is a 2011 recipient of the Romance Writers of America Centennial Award. Her career has focused on romantic suspense, often with paranormal elements.

Her 16 Berkley books and novellas include her nine-book werewolf "Moon" series. KILLING MOON was a launch book for the Berkley Sensation imprint. She has written for Harlequin, Berkley, Dell, Tor, Carina Press, Silhouette, Kensington, Running Press, Tudor, Pageant Books, and Scholastic.

Her many awards include two Rita finalist books. She has two Career Achievement awards from Romantic Times: for Series Romantic Suspense and for Series Romantic Mystery. And her Peregrine Connection series won a Lifetime Achievement Award for Romantic Suspense Series.

Many of her novels have been nominated for or won RT Reviewers Choice awards. In addition, she has won a Prism Award, several New Jersey Romance Writers Golden Leaf awards and numerous other awards.

Rebecca York loves to hear from readers!

Web site: http://www.rebeccayork.com
Email: rebecca@rebeccayork.com
Twitter: @rebeccayork43
Facebook: http://www.facebook.com/ruthglick
Blog: http://www.rebeccayork.blogspot.com

Sign up for Rebecca York's Newsletter to get all the scoop on Rebecca's
SEXY ROMANTIC SUSPENSE at
http://rebeccayork.com/for-readers/newsletter-sign-up/

CPSIA information can be obtained
at www.ICGtesting.com
Printed in the USA
LVOW10s1446120417

530575LV00013B/629/P